This book must be returned by the date specified at the time of issue as
the DATE DUE FOR RETURN.
The loan may be extended (personally, by post, telephone or online) for
a further period if the book is not required by another reader, by quoting
the above number / author / title.

Enquiries: 01709 336774

www.rotherham.gov.uk/libraries

ME

THE SPANISH GALLEON

Broken-hearted Madison Morley hopes Cornwall will be good for her soul. What she isn't expecting is to be pitched into a centuries-old mystery: the hunt for the treasure of a Spanish galleon. Accompanying her on her quest is Cornishman Luke Ryder, who is as handsome as he is exasperating. Can the couple work together to solve the clues and locate the galleon's fabled cargo? And will Madison discover something more precious than gold and silver along the way?

ELLIE HOLMES

THE SPANISH GALLEON

Complete and Unabridged

LINFORD
Leicester

First published in Great Britain in 2016

First Linford Edition
published 2017

A catalogue record for this book is available
from the British Library.

ISBN 978–1–4448–3258–7

Published by
F. A. Thorpe (Publishing)
Anstey, Leicestershire

Set by Words & Graphics Ltd.
Anstey, Leicestershire
Printed and bound in Great Britain by
T. J. International Ltd., Padstow, Cornwall

This book is printed on acid-free paper

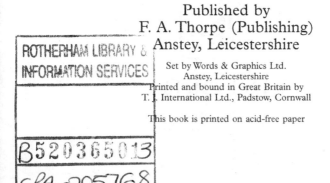

1

Madison Morley watched the quad bike pull up the steep hill that led from the Cornish fishing village of Penrowan to the railway station. As the bike crested the hill, the tone of the engine changed, and it arrived in the tiny lay-by outside the station with a roar of triumph.

The helmetless rider lifted Ray-Bans into his tangled blond hair. He wore cut-off cargo trousers and deck shoes, his white shirt billowing in the late-afternoon breeze. Madison could see he kept himself in good shape. He was in his early thirties at a guess; handsome in a rugged, outdoorsy kind of way.

'Miss Morley, I presume?'

Madison was taken aback. 'Yes,' she said, raising her hand against the dipping sun. 'But there must be some mistake. I'm waiting for a cab.'

There were deep grooves around the

man's eyes, hewn by the sun, which deepened still further as he smiled. 'That would be me.'

Madison's smile was slow and uncertain. 'You're kidding, right? Mrs Ryder said she'd send someone to pick me up...' The sentence died as the man's smile broadened. Come to think of it, Mrs Ryder hadn't actually used the word 'cab' in their brief conversation. 'You're my ride?'

'Yes, I am.'

'I can't get on that thing.'

' 'That thing' has a name,' he said, pretending to be affronted. 'Bessie. And she's perfectly safe.' His Cornish accent was rich and smooth, like warm honey.

She smiled. 'No offence to you or Bessie, but I think I'll get a proper cab.'

'Good luck with that.'

'If you could just give me the number of a local cab company?'

'I can give you the number, but it won't do you any good.'

She knew he was waiting for her to ask why. In the end, she gave in. 'Why?'

'Cars are banned from the village.'

Madison laughed out loud. Then she stopped laughing. He wasn't kidding. 'Seriously?'

He nodded. 'Seriously. Seems to me you have two options, Miss Morley. There's me and old Bessie, or there's Shanks's pony.'

She looked at the quad bike and then down at her clothes. She was wearing Gap jeans, a jumper, and spike-heeled boots.

'It's about a mile and a half to Mum's guest house,' he said as if reading her mind. 'But I guess it's a nice afternoon for a walk.'

What was that saying her grandfather used? In for a penny, in for a pound. She shrugged. How bad could it be?

Seeing that she was wavering, he twisted the throttle and the engine responded.

'Okay,' she said without enthusiasm.

'Stick the bag in the trailer and hop on.'

'The bag' was her treasured Stella

3

McCartney tote. Madison placed it with infinite care in the dusty trailer and looked for something to secure it with.

'Pull the tarp over it; it'll be fine.'

She gave the tarp a tug. The trailer looked ancient; its sides juddering alarmingly as the engine idled. One sharp corner or pothole and she had no doubt her precious tote would be bouncing along the road in their wake, the battered tarp flying along behind it.

'Meter's been running since I got here, love. Are you getting on or not?'

'Meter?' She raised an incredulous eyebrow. 'You think I'm going to pay to ride on that thing? You should be paying me.'

He laughed; a deep chortle of joy that seemed to rise from his belly and explode upwards and outwards. 'Fair point. Anyway, I was pulling your leg. It's free for anyone staying at Harbour Watch.'

He said it like it was a perk. Other places had complimentary toiletries and soft, fluffy bathrobes. This place came with a death-trap jalopy and a clown. Just her luck!

'I don't suppose there's a helmet?'

'I appear to have left them at home, sorry.' He didn't sound sorry.

Madison swung her leg over the seat and looked for somewhere to hold on to. There was no grab handle behind the seat. She could reach back and hold on to the edge of the trailer, but she hated to think what that would be like on the move.

'All aboard?' he called over his shoulder.

'Yes.' She hitched her legs up and tensed her thighs against the bike. Maybe that and sheer willpower would be enough to keep her seated.

'Get a grip!' he commanded.

'Of what?'

'Me!'

With a roar they leapt forward. Madison tilted backwards and then slammed into the man's back as they pitched out onto the steep hill that led down into the village. She wound her arms around his waist with alacrity.

'I don't even know your name,' she shouted against the onrushing wind.

'Luke Ryder. Pleased to meet you.'

*   *   *

Penrowan was everything Madison's grandfather had said it was: fishermen's pastel-coloured cottages clustered around an ancient harbour, steep wooded hillsides rising up on either side with the sea filling the mouth of the valley, a radiant blue in the last of the afternoon sun. Madison could see why cars were banned. They would never be able to negotiate Penrowan's narrow lanes.

As Luke eased the bike to a halt, Madison took in her surroundings. Home was a metropolitan sprawl of concrete, choked with traffic and people; an assault on the senses. Here, the land was soft and lush and wondrously green, the sea a shade of blue she had thought only possible in the Mediterranean. She watched the water lap lazily at the harbour wall. It was so clear that she could see a starfish

6

on the sandy sea floor. Taking a deep breath, she filled her lungs with the fresh, invigorating scent of the sea, and felt the tension and fatigue of her journey slip away.

'It's beautiful,' she said.

'Yeah, I guess it is,' Luke agreed, sounding surprised at the thought. 'Sometimes I wish I could see it through a visitor's eyes,' he added, a touch wistfully.

Madison marvelled at the idea that anyone could become inured to this landscape.

'Welcome to Harbour Watch.' He spread his arm to indicate the house to their right.

Harbour Watch stood on a slight incline metres from the entrance to the harbour. Three storeys of whitewashed stone; each window framed by smart navy-blue shutters offset by blue window boxes planted with jaunty cream primroses. At ground level there was a giant garage door. It and the front door were also painted blue. A slate name plate depicted the curve of the hills and a sturdy house standing front

and centre to the harbour with the words
'Harbour Watch' picked out in beautiful
italic script.

Madison realised that she had continued to hug Luke Ryder the whole time
she had been studying Harbour Watch.
A little embarrassed, she now let go and
gave him a wry smile. 'Thanks, I guess.'

He smiled back. 'Not as bad as you
thought, right?'

'Well...' She waggled her hand in a
'jury's still out on that one, pal' kind of
way.

He reached round, flicked the tarp
back, and swung her tote from the
trailer. 'There's a cream tea waiting for
you. Better be warned, Mum will have
your life story before you've finished
your scone.'

Madison grinned as she drew her
mobile from her pocket.

'You won't get a signal down here.
Black spot in the valley. You need to head
back up the hill to where I picked you
up for a decent signal. Failing that, you
can always give the phone rock a try, but

it really depends which way the wind's blowing.'

'The phone rock?'

'Up on the headland.' He pointed to the cliff to their right. 'The cliff path starts behind the Green Man pub. If you stand on the big flat rock on the peak and face west, you can sometimes get a signal. Wind's in the right direction today. Have fun.'

With that he was gone, roaring up the lane and out of sight.

2

'You must be Madison! Welcome to Harbour Watch. I hope Luke was on his best behaviour.'

Madison smiled politely, unsure how to answer that. What was his worst like?

'I'm Kathryn Ryder,' the older lady said, and reached for Madison's bag. 'Let me get that for you.'

'Oh please, Mrs Ryder, there's no need.'

'Nonsense. You're a guest. I don't let guests carry their own bags! Where does that end — make your own breakfast and while you're at it make the bed? No, no, no, and it's Kathryn. Mrs Ryder was my mum, God rest her soul, and she's residing in Penrowan churchyard.'

As Kathryn was talking, she led Madison in through the wide front door. Madison was surprised to find there was no ground floor as such to the house, just a huge storage area. Behind the massive garage door were two motorboats. The largest, *Peggy's Pride*, had a cabin in the middle and seemed to be undergoing some sort of renovation. Next to it was a second, smaller motorboat called *Kathryn's Pride*. It had seats at the front and a driver's console to one side at the back. Against the wall, Madison could see canoes, diving equipment and fishing paraphernalia.

'Luke keeps all his junk here,' Kathryn said.

'Does he live here?'

'No, he's got a cottage up Pennycombe Lane, but tain't big enough for all his stuff.' Kathryn guided her towards a set of stairs at the back.

'It's very generous of you to give over a whole floor of your house,' Madison said.

'That's just the way it was built, my lovely. Only the second-home owners and the people from up country live on the ground floor this close to the harbour. See the way the floor slopes?' Madison nodded. 'It's so that the sea can wash back out.'

11

The chunky steps were made of stone and painted white with dips in the centre, from centuries of boots clumping up them, Madison imagined. About a third of the way up, the treads changed to wood.

'Last winter the worst storm we had was a sevener,' Kathryn said, pointing to the seventh stair as an indication of how high the water had risen. 'Never had a niner in my lifetime, but Mum saw the like. Frightening it was, so she said. Never underestimate the power of water.'

Madison looked back the way they had come. 'My grandfather won't be able to make the stairs, Mrs ... Kathryn. I'll still stay, of course, but I'll need to find somewhere else for him.'

'Donnee worry, my lovely. Your grandfather's going to stay up Pennycombe with Luke. Pennycombe's got a rise to it and Luke's half way up, but there's nice level access directly outside the property. Well...' She laughed. 'As level as you'll find in Cornwall. Ground-floor bedroom, en-suite bathroom. All mod cons. Nice little terrace at the back to watch the world go by, catch a bit of sun. Luke'll take good care of him.'

Madison had her reservations about that, but then an even graver concern took precedence, and she wondered why she hadn't thought of it earlier. 'I'm not sure how my grandfather is going to make it down into the village. He's flying into Newquay tomorrow, and there's a cab bringing him here — leastways ...'

'All taken care of,' Kathryn assured her.

'But he's got a very bad hip. He needs an operation.'

'The Prof and I had a long chat. I know what the score is.' Kathryn patted Madison's arm.

'But the quad bike ...'

'Luke is going to make some modifications ready for when he picks the Prof up.'

Madison's mind boggled. 'He really is very delicate.'

Kathryn smiled kindly. 'The Prof's a lot tougher than you think.'

'You know him?'

Kathryn laughed. 'Everyone knows the Prof. He's an honorary Penrowanian. By hook or by crook, we'll get him up Pennycombe. Donnee worry! I'll show you up to your room.'

'Thank you.'

Madison followed Kathryn through a hallway and up another flight of stairs, carpeted this time. The second-floor landing was wide and airy, with a sash window complete with window seat overlooking the harbour. Madison paused to admire the view as Kathryn unlocked the door to Madison's left. 'I'll leave you to settle in, my lovely,' Kathryn said as she handed Madison her key. 'Come down to the kitchen when you're ready. Next floor down, door to the right. I'll pop the kettle on.'

'Thank you so much.'

Madison's room was a generous size. The double bed had a white wooden frame and soft blue and white bedding. There was a small wardrobe plus a chest of drawers. On the bedside table Kathryn had stood a vase of purple, yellow and red tulips. They provided a wonderful pop of colour against the whitewashed wall. Madison took a moment to admire the collection of summery Cornish seascapes that adorned the walls; a local artist no doubt, their love of the scenery singing out from every brushstroke.

Depositing her tote on the bed, Madison drifted to the window. The large sash had blue curtains pulled back by rope ties and a window seat fashioned from blue and white cotton ticking. The foam seat was wide and deep, the cushions just right. You could lose hours here and never be bored watching the boats bob on the water, the gulls diving and the tourists strolling by, Madison thought.

I'm going to be happy here. The thought surprised her. What an odd feeling to have. She was only staying for a few days.

It was an effort to move away from the window and continue her exploration of her room. The en-suite was small but clean and tidy, with a selection of Molton Brown toiletries. A fluffy bathrobe hung on a hook on the back of the door. So, the death-trap jalopy and the clown weren't the only extras after all.

Thinking of Luke, Madison frowned. He seemed like the type of guy who didn't take life too seriously. She wasn't at all sure she wanted to entrust her beloved grandfather to his care, either on a perilous trip from the top of the hill or in his cottage. But it would be impossible to make other arrangements now without hurting Kathryn's feelings, and she knew she couldn't do that. She suspected Luke's feelings would be a little harder to hurt. He'd probably just shrug his broad shoulders and amble off.

Madison found herself back at the window as if pulled there by an invisible cord. She watched the water lap at the stone walls of the harbour, making the boats tip and roll in the current. She couldn't tell if the tide was coming in or going out, but it seemed pretty high.

She sighed. What was this weird feeling that was pervading her body? Contentment? Wow, where had that come from? She had been running so hard for so long, she had almost forgotten what it felt like.

First there had been the break-up with Will. One minute they'd been signing the lease on an apartment on the Lower East Side in New York, the next she'd been packing boxes to move out. At least, that was how it had seemed. Three years had flown by in the blink of an eye. The man she had married had turned out to be a flawed individual.

'We're all flawed,' her mum had said.

Her parents had liked Will. By the end, they'd liked him more than she did.

Then her coveted job at the Museum of Modern Art in New York had crashed and burned. 'I'm real sorry, Madison,' her manager had told her. 'Budgets are constricted. I gotta let you go.'

She'd been devastated; but, to be honest, she probably couldn't have afforded to stay in New York on her conservator's salary without waitressing in the evenings and cleaning in the mornings. It wasn't that she was afraid of hard work; it just wasn't how she'd planned to spend her life.

And then her grandfather had called, with impeccable timing as always. 'Got myself in a bit of bother, old Stick,' he'd said. 'I've just got back from a research trip to Machu Picchu. I need to get all my papers and photographs in order so I can start my next book. Total chaos, as always. You know how it is.'

She knew. Papers everywhere: spilling out of folders and files, piled high on every available flat surface, reference books open on the furniture and the windowsill. The disarray always reached its height at the start of every new book, diminishing, if only ever so slightly, by the end of it.

The study in her grandfather's west London home was her favourite room in the whole world: floor-to-ceiling bookshelves, antique green leather Chesterfields, and the biggest desk she had ever seen. As a child she had liked to sit under it reading while her grandfather worked diligently above. She had passed many happy hours devouring Enid Blyton adventures as the dust motes danced in the air around her.

There had always been quite a lot of dust due to the cleaner being banned from entering the room, just like everyone else, unless they had express permission from the Prof. The study was his sanctuary, his office, and the anchor that pulled him home from his many far-flung trips.

'Heard you might be at a bit of a loose end,' he'd said to Madison, 'and I wondered if I could impose? You've probably got tons of things you'd rather be doing than helping me.'

She hadn't. Was that good or bad? She couldn't decide.

'Best research assistant I ever had.'

'I'd love to come.'

'I'll wire the money for the ticket.'

'You don't have to do that, Pop!'

'Part of the deal, Sticky Stick!'

She couldn't remember when he'd started calling her Stick, but it had stuck. He'd told her when she'd asked about the nickname's derivation that he had once likened her to a stick insect when he'd realised just how much she'd grown between visits.

'You had these long, thin limbs shooting out, getting longer and longer, like me and your Dad. Not that good for a girl,' he'd conceded. 'Cuts down the gene pool. Little men will run away as quick as their tiny legs can carry them,' he'd said with a chuckle. 'Still, never mind. No man will ever be good enough for Sticky Stick!'

And so it had proved thus far. She still lived in hope. Hope rather than expectation, she had to admit. She'd thought Will was the one. How wrong could she have been?

It was only when she had touched down at Heathrow, and her grandfather had whisked her away for afternoon tea at the Thames Foyer in the Savoy, that he'd admitted he needed an operation.

'Doc says my left hip is for the knackers' yard. Too many miles on the clock. Too many miles climbing blinking mountains. Still, rather go to my grave with a whole load of silicone in my joints than have to sit on my backside never going anywhere. I've told the Doc I need to go back to Machu Picchu in the autumn. He says if I want to do that, I need to book myself in soonest. It's no big deal. Up and about in no time, but I make a terrible patient. I'm never ill, so I get no practice! You'll cheer me up, won't you, Stick? We'll have a jolly time sorting all my papers. I'll be the most organised I've ever been.'

Madison had barely settled in when the letter postmarked Penrowan had arrived, throwing all their plans skyward. It had turned out it wasn't so much a letter as an SOS. She'd watched, with growing concern, as the colour had drained out of her grandfather's face at the breakfast table. 'Pop, what's wrong?'

Her grandfather gazed into the middle distance, eyes unfocused.

'Pop?'

'We need to go to Penrowan. Today!'

'Where's Penrowan?'

'It's on the south Cornish coast.'

'Today?' It was the squeak of disbelief

21

in her voice that had brought his attention back to the table.

'Absolutely. I'll make the arrangements. We can travel down by plane later today. Get a flight into Newquay. We can get a taxi from there. No, wait! I'll need my papers. You can travel down today. I'll meet you down there. The papers I need are in storage. I can request they be delivered first thing tomorrow, then I'll follow on.'

'What's all this about, Pop?'

A smile touched his lips, lightening the look of worry that had fallen across his face. 'A girl I once knew — a woman now, of course.' He sighed. 'Miranda Catesby. We were inseparable for eighteen wonderful months when we were teenagers. Our friendship was bookended by two of the most perfect summers I think I've ever experienced. Or maybe that's just what youth does to you, lengthening out the salad days in your mind so that no other day quite captures that magic again.'

Conscious that he was growing wistful, Madison sought to steer him back on course. 'The letter is from Miranda?' she prompted, indicating the envelope still clutched in his hand.

He looked down at it as if surprised to find he was still holding it. 'Yes, both letters.'

'Both?'

'When I got back from Peru there was a letter from Miranda waiting for me. I knew her handwriting immediately even after all these years. Heaven knows how she knew where to write. My publisher, I suppose. I hadn't seen or heard from her in years. You can imagine, therefore, that I read her letter with some trepidation.'

'What did it say?' Madison asked eagerly.

'She said she'd been having some work done at Catesby Hall. In the process they had found a priest hole that had been bricked up long ago. Inside was a wooden chest full of papers. She was sure the papers would finally lead her to the Spanish galleon.

'The galleon was a near-fabled ship we'd spent those two long summers hunting for. It was what had taken me to Cornwall in the first place. Miranda's three-times great-grandfather Milton Catesby had been one of the Victorian plant-hunters. Splendid fellow. Trekked all over South America. The subtropical garden at Catesby Hall still retains some of his discoveries, flourishing in the mild climate. Anyway, Milton published several journals, and in one of them he talked about the Spanish galleon.

'He described it in loving detail. 'This castle of the sea' is what he called it, for that's how it would have looked: three decks high with three or four masts, sails billowing. It would've been an imposing sight, but its strength was also its downfall. Because of its size, its manoeuvrability was poor. Caught in the ravages of a Cornish storm, hundreds of nautical miles off course, and laden with treasure, passengers and cargo, it was blown onto the rocks at Penrowan in 1567. A jagged hole was ripped in its side and it sank. A handful of sailors made it to shore with tales of the treasure on board.

'I was a dreamer then, a romantic. My head was full of the treasure waiting to be discovered in the wreck of the galleon. I press-ganged Miranda into my search, though truth be told, she needed very little persuasion.' He smiled, wreathed in memories.

'I'm guessing you didn't find it,' Madison said gently.

'You are correct, my dear. Despite our very best efforts, the galleon eluded us. It took on a mythical status in our minds. We conceded an honourable defeat.'

'And then, all these years later, Miranda Catesby writes to you out of the blue to say she's resuming the search?'

The Professor nodded. 'I don't believe the Catesby family ever stopped looking, not really, but Miranda and I both felt some vital pieces of the puzzle were missing. Then Miranda found this chest of papers and clearly thought she was on the verge of a breakthrough. She promised to keep me updated.'

'How exciting!' Madison declared.

'And what does today's letter say?' she asked eagerly. 'Has she found it?'

The frown returned to his face. 'I fear something has gone terribly wrong,' he said sombrely. 'It is not her handwriting on the envelope, so she clearly got someone else to post it. Inside is a paper napkin, the sort you use on a picnic and then discard. She's scrawled a message to me in lipstick, quickly I'd say, judging by the messy nature of the letters. Miranda always had such a clear hand.'

'What does it say?'

The Professor held the napkin aloft. Madison gasped. The letters daubed untidily in scarlet read, 'Help me.'

'This Miranda Catesby was very dear to you once?' Madison guessed.

The Professor nodded. 'No offence to your beloved, departed grandmother, but Miranda Catesby was the love of my life.'

Madison was moved by the expression on her grandfather's face. 'So I guess I'd better go and pack.'

'I'll ring the Doc. Put him off for

a week or so until we find out what's going on.'

Madison nodded. She knew it was pointless trying to talk him out of it.

'You'll love Penrowan, Maddy. It's the kind of place that's good for the soul. Soothing.'

Now, staring out of the sash window at the bustling harbour, Madison could not agree more. Then she remembered how her grandfather's eyes had narrowed as he'd looked at her. 'And I suspect, after all you've been through lately, your soul is in need of a bit soothing, eh, Stick?'

Madison smiled. Her grandfather was one smart guy.

⋆ ⋆ ⋆

Luke Ryder sat on the wooden bench high up on the headland and stared out over the indigo sea. On the horizon, fingers of slate-grey cloud heralded the rain that was due overnight. The wind was up, blowing the rainclouds in. He could taste the tangy salt of the sea on his lips,

27

and the familiar pull of grief made his stomach drop. Twelve years on and it was still as raw. Sure, he covered it up well, but the damage had not been made good; never could be. Like a shoddy builder, he had skimmed the gap with jokes and a devil-may-care attitude, but it was a thin layer of plaster to disguise the yawning hole beneath.

He was getting maudlin. It was all this trouble with his ma. He hated the thought of her facing more pain. Those damn Catesbys! How he wished there was some way he could make it all right. She didn't deserve the worry they were piling on her. Maybe the Prof could suggest something. He'd bend his ear over a couple of beers. The Prof had known Miranda Catesby back along. Yeah, that would be a good way to go. Feeling better about the situation, Luke looked down at his sketchpad.

He'd caught that look of annoyance and incredulity on her face and was pleased with it. He didn't get to draw people as much as he would have liked.

He studied his work. Her long hair was flowing around her shoulders, and large eyes were glowing and beautiful, even in this simple pencil sketch. Imagine what it would look like when he worked it up in watercolours: the tumble of auburn hair, thick and glossy, with a touch of vermillion to show her spirit, and emerald green for her eyes.

He glanced up. The subject of his drawing was a couple of hundred yards away, scrambling up the rocks to stand atop the rock he'd pointed out to her from the harbour. He watched her unashamedly, knowing that the steep curve of the hill and the lush greenery all around him would shield him from her view.

Damn, she was beautiful. Her hair streaked out, whipped around by the wind. Her clothes were being painted against her by the approaching weather front. He watched as out of her pocket she took her phone, dutifully turned to the west, and held it up hopefully to the sky.

At this point, he'd normally start to chuckle. The phone rock was always good for a laugh; a trick to play on gullible tourists so wedded to their interconnected lives that they couldn't stand the stress of living with no bars on their phones. He'd never owned a mobile, so he struggled to understand their addiction. But something about Madison's anguish touched him and killed the joke. She seemed genuinely distressed about the lack of signal, not just angry like the others had been.

Luke hadn't wanted to cause her pain. He kicked himself for that and, ashamed, thrust his sketchbook away. Turning, he climbed the hill and headed into the village along the back way.

3

When Madison drew back the curtains, it was as though Penrowan had been freshly laundered and hung out to dry after last night's rain. The pastel-coloured cottages stood out brightly against the lush green hillsides. Their damp slate roofs were several shades darker after the drenching, streaked with blue and purple. It looked more like a movie set than a genuine village.

But real life was all about her: in the boy on his bicycle delivering papers, laundry flapping on lines in the steep back gardens, and in the harbour itself, where fishermen called out to each other from squat vessels as diesel engines spluttered into life.

Madison craned her neck. The sky was blue and cloudless. The knot of worry in her stomach worked its way out. As she'd settled down last night, warm and comfortable with the soft quilt a cloud around her shoulders, she had been soothed to sleep by the sound of the lashing rain, though not before she had whispered a quick prayer that it would be dry in the morning for her grandfather's arrival.

She showered and dressed, choosing a pair of white cotton trousers and a blue and white striped Breton-style sweater. She knew the weather well enough to know it could change in the blink of an eye, and also that this time of year, however bright and sunny, there was likely to be a chill in the air.

She could hear voices as she went down to breakfast, and suppressed a sigh. Luke Ryder first thing in the morning was likely to be a challenge. She thrust back the kitchen door with an air of confidence she did not feel.

The room was bright and airy, with a slate floor and white wooden units. The oven was a dark blue monster of an Aga with a huge pot of utensils beside it. A tray of herbs stood on the wide kitchen windowsill and copper-bottomed pans hung from a rack over the scrubbed pine table. It was clear to see this was a real cook's kitchen, and the smell of frying bacon made Madison's stomach growl.

Luke and his mother were seated at the table, deep in conversation, as Madison entered. She picked up on the atmosphere right away; the tension was as pungent as the sizzling bacon. 'Is everything okay?' she asked cautiously.

They looked up from the papers scattered over the table, and Kathryn's frown instantly dissolved into a smile. Luke's smile was slower to arrive and quicker to leave as he gathered the papers together and thrust them into a canvas bag that was hanging from the back of his chair.

'Did you sleep well, my lovely?' Kathryn asked.

'I had the most amazing sleep,' Madison admitted. 'I thought it'd take me ages to drop off, but snuggled down in that warm, cosy bed listening to the rain, I was gone in seconds.'

'That'll be the sea air,' Kathryn said,

rising to tend to the bacon. 'I've got a full English on the go for Luke. I'll do the same for you. Sit down. There's tea in the pot. English Breakfast, but there's Darjeeling in the cupboard if you'd prefer. Hold on, would you like a coffee? I've a percolator; I could brew you a cup?'

'Tea will be fine,' Madison assured her.

Luke poured the tea for her and added a splash of milk. There was a bowl of sugar cubes on the table but she shook her head. The tea was hot and strong and just what she needed.

'So your mother cooks you breakfast?' Madison raised her eyebrows at Luke across the table. 'Tell me, does she do your laundry too?' She smiled.

'It may surprise you to know I wash my own socks. I usually cook my own breakfast too, but today's different.' He clapped his hands together. 'The Prof's coming.'

Madison nodded. She was just about to question him on the dreaded modifications to the quad bike when two plates of Full English arrived on the table.

Madison had had a cooked breakfast on many occasions, but she'd never seen a plate quite so full. The sausage was plump and rich, and next to it were three slices of bacon, cooked to perfection. There was also a giant mushroom, glossy fried tomatoes, a thick slice of buttered home-made bread which had been toasted and crowned with a fried egg, and a little ramekin of baked beans. Madison wasn't altogether sure whether she was supposed to deposit the beans onto the plate or eat them from the dish. The food looked and smelt delicious, even if this grand display made the coffee and croissant she normally started the day with look stingy.

'All the ingredients are local, none of that mass-produced rubbish. Eat what you like, leave the rest,' Kathryn said, touching Madison's shoulder and smiling. 'I guarantee that by the end of the week, after you've tramped up and down these Cornish hills a few times, you'll be pol-ishing off a full plate every day,' she said with a wink.

Madison had her doubts about that,

but gamely took up her knife and fork and tucked in. Luke poured them both a glass of fresh orange juice without asking and nudged it towards her. 'No bits. Can't stand bits.'

'Thanks.'

She watched him tip the dish of beans over the top of his egg and squish them into the yolk so that an orangey-yellow liquid dripped off his toast. Madison delicately tipped hers out over the mushroom.

'I did what you suggested yesterday, but I couldn't get a signal.' Was that a guilty look she caught on Luke's face?

Kathryn slapped him with her tea towel. 'Luke! You didn't send her up to the phone rock? I'm sorry, Madison. Sometimes I don't think he progressed beyond the age of twelve. There are no mobile signals anywhere in the village. You have to be up at the station for your phone to work. But you're welcome to use the phone in the hall anytime you like. I hope yesterday's call wasn't important?'

'I just wanted to check on Pop.'

Kathryn smiled. 'The Prof can take care of himself better than any of us here, including Luke.' She flicked the cloth at her son once more. 'You and that phone rock!' She tutted and walked out.

'Sorry about that,' Luke mumbled, head down as he continued to devour his breakfast.

Madison had never seen anyone eat so fast. 'Why did you do it?' she asked, genuinely mystified.

He shrugged — a seven-year-old caught with his hand in the cookie jar and no one else to blame. She thought about the boys she'd grown up with in London laughing at the tourists studying their maps, delighting in sending them in the opposite direction to their destination. She guessed all communities had their ways of enjoying themselves at the expense of outsiders.

'Well, I might not have got a signal, but I did get a terrific view from up there,' she said, eager to build a bridge. This man would have her grandfather's safety in his hands later today. She needed him on side.

He looked up and smiled. 'Yeah, it is pretty amazing up there, isn't it?'

She nodded and returned to her food. Luke was mopping up the last of the eggy explosion from his plate with a thick slice of wholemeal bread when Madison conceded defeat. A third of her plate remained untouched. She hoped Kathryn wouldn't be offended.

As her hostess returned to the kitchen carrying the post, Madison said, 'That was delicious, Kathryn, but I —'

'No need to explain. I told you, my dear.' The plate was whisked away.

Luke smiled at her. 'We reckoned you'd only eat half.'

Madison was pleased she had beaten their expectations, even if she was feeling uncomfortably full right now.

'Personally, I hate a woman who picks at her food. I had a girlfriend once who thought a couple of leaves of lettuce and a slice of cucumber was a meal. Why are you looking at me like that?'

'I'm just adjusting to the idea of you having a girlfriend,' she deadpanned, keen to get her own back after the phone rock incident.

He took her ribbing in good humour, a smile nudging at his lips. 'More than one, actually.'

'You don't say? Any of them stick around for a second date?' She smiled sweetly.

'Two of them married me.'

That floored her.

'What time is the Prof arriving?' he asked.

'He should be here at ten.'

'Cool. I'll meet you downstairs.'

★ ★ ★

'No way!'

'He'll be fine.'

'Is that thing even legal?' Madison asked, her voice rising in indignation.

'I carry the Carnival Queen around on it every year, and not one of them has ever come a cropper.'

'It's an armchair on a trailer,' Madison said. She peered more closely. 'Oh my God, it's got wheels!' She'd experienced Luke's liking for speed and could just imagine the trailer hitting a bump in the road, the back end falling down, and the armchair with her grandfather strapped inside sailing down the steep hill at Pennycombe and into the cool water of the harbour. 'No, no, no!'

Luke stood outside his mother's house with his toned arms folded, an infuriating smirk on his face.

'This isn't funny!' she shouted.

'No, it's not.'

'Then why are you smirking?'

'Because you're funny. Very funny, when you're angry. There are little red spots of rage on your cheeks and your green eyes have gone several shades darker. How in the world do you do that?'

Madison didn't know how to respond, which made her angrier still.

'Look, Maddy, it's obvious —'

'Madison,' she corrected him imperiously.

He re-set his mouth in a doomed attempt to hide his smile, which was already well established in his eyes. 'Sorry, Madison,' he said, not sounding the least bit sorry as he emphasised her name.

She had never wanted to do anyone physical harm before, not even Will, but Luke Ryder was pushing her close.

'You care about your grandfather. We all do. The Prof is a legend in the village. No one wants to see the old guy come to any harm, least of all me. I wouldn't suggest it if I wasn't one hundred percent sure he'd be fine. Why don't we let the Prof decide when he gets here? If he's not keen, we can maybe help him onto the seat behind me. In the meantime, let me take you for a test drive and prove to you how safe it is.'

Madison's eyes narrowed. If there were a chance her grandfather would consent to riding in this contraption, she owed it to him to have at least tried it out first. Reluctantly, she nodded.

'Good.' He unhooked the bolts at the back of the trailer to lower the tailgate and then held out his hand to her. 'My lady...'

Ignoring his outstretched hand, Madison climbed aboard the trailer, one hand on the arm of the chair, which was made of oxblood-red leather. Tentatively, she lowered herself into the chair. She had to admit it was very soft and very comfortable, if perhaps a little low for her grandfather in his current state. She tested how secure the seat was by bracing her feet against the floor of the trailer and trying to move it. The chair had a little give against its rope constraints, but nowhere near as much as she'd feared.

'Pretty good, huh?'

'Jury's still out, buster.'

He grinned. 'Will you allow me to strap you in?'

She agreed, mostly because she wasn't entirely sure how the strap worked. Luke jumped up into the trailer, making the whole thing rattle alarmingly; but even with his added weight, the arm-chair hardly moved at all. Madison was secretly impressed but determined not to show it. From behind and from the sides, Luke wrapped a four-way strap around her, securing all the strands in a chunky stainless-steel clasp. She heard a satisfying clunk as all the straps were pushed home.

'I borrowed it when the funfair came to Tregelian,' Luke said, 'and forgot to give it back.' He winked. 'Safe as houses.' He patted the belt.

'Drive slow!' she commanded.

'Of course, dear.'

She felt a bit of an idiot as Luke circled round and headed down the main road of Penrowan and out towards the railway station, but she reminded herself she was doing this for her grandfather's benefit. Luke, for once, was keeping the throttle under control, and they were moving along at a pedestrian pace. As they passed by, various villagers gave them a cheery wave, calling out to Luke.

Madison felt herself begin to relax. In fact, she was even beginning to enjoy the ride. Then they got to the steep pull-up to the station car park and Madison's doubts crowded back. The tone of the quad bike's engine changed, and Madison felt Luke adjust the throttle. The injection of power vibrating through her, combined with the angle of the trailer, made Madison feel a little nauseous. She had to admit, though, that even at its steepest, the armchair hardly moved at all. She was nevertheless relieved when they arrived at the station.

'Okay?' Luke asked. The cocky smile was gone, replaced by a look of genuine concern.

She nodded. 'It wasn't as bad as I thought,' she said.

'Praise indeed!' He helped her down with a grin.

The hotelier from across the way waved a greeting from his front porch. 'Come to get the Prof, Luke?'

Luke nodded.

'Righto, I'll get the stuff you asked for.'

Madison raised an enquiring eyebrow at Luke, who refused to meet her gaze.

The hotelier disappeared inside and then reappeared, carrying two pillows and a set of wooden steps. Luke settled the pillows onto the seat of the armchair and placed the wooden steps at the end of the trailer. 'Thanks, Mick. I'll let you have them back when the Prof goes home.'

'No problem.'

Luke turned to Madison. 'I figured the Prof might need a hand getting into the trailer; and with his hip and all, he might appreciate sitting a little higher.'

Madison was touched. 'Good thinking.'

'We use the steps on the beach at Tregelian in the season so the little ones can climb on the donkeys. Not much call for them this time of year, so the Prof is welcome to use them,' Mick said.

'Thank you,' Madison said. She held out her hand. 'I'm —'

'Madison Morley, the Profs grand-daughter. Yeah, I know. The Prof's told us all about you over the years. Kept asking him to bring you down to visit us but he never did. Glad to finally make your acquaintance. You're every bit as beautiful as the Prof said you were.'

Madison blushed.

'When are you planning to finish my decorating, Luke? I need to get that back wall done before the season starts.'

'Dreckly, Mick.'

Mick laughed. 'Sometime between now and Christmas then. I need it done by Easter, Luke. No messing.'

'It will be.'

They all turned as a cab pulled up. Professor Compton Morley was so deep in conversation with the driver that several minutes passed before the cab door opened and a wooden cane with a silver top appeared, closely followed by a tall, spare man with white hair and a full white beard. The driver took the Professor's suitcase from the boot and shook the Professor warmly by the hand. They exchanged a few more words before the driver set off with a toot of his horn.

'Fascinating fellow,' the Prof said. 'Volunteers two weeks a year with the VSO. He's just come back from Sierra Leone. Sticky Stick! You look amazing. I see the Cornish air has put a bloom in your cheeks already. Luke, my boy, how the devil are you?' The Prof grabbed Luke by the hand and shook it vigorously.

'I'm very well, Professor.'

The Prof turned to Mick. 'Michael, good to see you, too!'

'And you, Professor.'

'Now, what on earth have we got here?' he said, surveying the seat on the trailer.

'Your carriage awaits, Professor.'

Luke held out his hand to help the Professor up the steps.

The older man laughed loudly. 'While I loathe making any concessions to my damn hip, I have to say I'm prepared to make an exception on this occasion, given that I shall travel in such style and that you have clearly gone to a lot of trouble on my behalf.'

'No trouble, Professor,' Luke assured him. He stowed his passenger's suitcase at the side of the trailer, wedging it in firmly, and then set about strapping the Professor in. He grinned at Madison as he climbed aboard the quad bike and turned the throttle. 'You'll be okay to walk, Maddy, won't you?'

He didn't wait for her reply as he pulled out of the station car park to a yelp of delight and an exuberant cry of 'Tally Ho!' from her grandfather as he waved his stick aloft.

4

Madison followed the directions Kathryn had given her to Luke's home and found Rock Cottage halfway up Pennycombe Lane. Two fishermen's cottages knocked together, it was a broad-fronted, solidly built dwelling. The stone had received a recent coat of whitewash by the look of it. There were two sash windows on the upper floor and one at ground level. The navy-blue front door stood ajar.

Madison knocked and stepped inside. The lounge was cosy, with a squashy sofa and two chairs upholstered in blues and creams arranged around a slate fireplace inside which was an ornate glass-fronted log-burner. Above the massive oak beam that formed the mantelpiece was a splendid painting of a storm-lashed Penrowan harbour. A flat-screen TV stood discreetly in one corner. In the other was a bookcase crammed with books. Madison needed to recalibrate. This was not the bachelor pad she had been expecting.

She closed the front door behind her and followed the sound of laughter into a modern, bright and airy kitchen diner, and then out onto a wooden terrace suspended over the water that ran like a deck around the perimeter of the property. Here she found her grandfather and Kathryn. Luke was nowhere in sight.

Madison was pleased to see her grandfather ensconced in an upholstered teak chair looking none the worse for his trip into the village. He was now wearing a panama hat and twirling his silver-topped cane as he took in the panoramic view of the harbour.

'Best spot in Penrowan,' he declared. He grinned at Madison and motioned for her to join him, indicating the spare chair to his left. 'Don't you agree, Stick?'

It really was quite magnificent. Situated to the left of the harbour, Rock Cottage enabled its inhabitants to see right around the horseshoe-shaped harbour and then back out to sea. 'It is beautiful,' she said.

'Are you okay?' she asked her grandfather, her hand on his shoulder as she sat.

'Capital, dear girl. The ride on Bessie was terrific. Luke has promised to take me for a spin around the village later so I can say hello to some old friends.'

'We're having a cream tea,' Kathryn said, indicating the plate of scones on the table. 'Would you like to join us, Madison?'

Madison had smelt the scones baking in Kathryn's kitchen just prior to her grandfather's arrival and had envied Kathryn's skill as a baker. Despite that, she hesitated. It was her second cream tea in as many days, but Kathryn's eager smile made it impossible to refuse.

Nodding, Madison banished the thought that she was going to put pounds on during this stay, and watched as Kathryn poured the tea from a stout brown pot into a brightly glazed blue mug. Then she split a scone and piled first strawberry jam and then a generous dollop of clotted cream on top.

It was a miracle to Madison how the

people of Cornwall were not all clinically obese. She guessed it was the punishingly steep hills they had to traverse. You had no choice but to be fit if you lived here. Nevertheless, she feared for their arteries.

'Do you know what makes a Cornish cream tea Cornish, as opposed to a Devon cream tea?' her grandfather asked.

'No.' Madison took a bite of her scone. Light and fluffy, it tasted heavenly.

'The Cornish put the jam on first and then the cream. The people of Devon do it the other way round,' he said.

Kathryn tsked with her tongue at the thought of such an abomination.

'The Cornish way is the right way,' her grandfather said, smiling indulgently at Kathryn.

'The Cornish way is the *only* way,' she said firmly.

Madison took another bite of the scone. She didn't really see the importance of which came first, the juicy jam or the gloriously rich cream. All she knew for certain was that when put together, it was naughtily delicious.

'From Knowledown Farm?' the Prof asked.

Kathryn nodded. 'Pete and his wife, Denny, decided to diversify a few years ago. Now they make their own jam in a variety of flavours,' she said for Madison's benefit. 'They also churn their own butter and make ice cream, cream, and Cornish brie. They opened up a little shop beside the dairy. Best decision they ever made, so Denny says.'

Madison chased a dribble of jam with her finger and caught Luke grinning at her from the doorway.

'Ah, I see my chauffeur has arrived. Tucked Bessie safely away?' the Prof asked.

'I have,' Luke said.

'Tea and scone, Luke?' his mother asked.

'Please. So, what do you think of Rock Cottage?' Luke asked, looking across at Madison.

'I think it's beautiful,' she said without hesitation. She was happy to tease and goad him, but there was no point being coy about a property as gorgeous as this one.

He nodded in contented agreement as he accepted a mug of tea from his mother.

'Well, my dears, to business,' the Prof said. He told Kathryn and Luke about Miranda Catesby's first letter.

'The Spanish galleon?' Luke whistled. 'I thought that was an old wives' tale.'

'I was of much the same opinion, my boy, especially after spending two fruitless summers chasing after it. There wasn't an inch of water between here and Tregelian that Miranda and I did not search. We scuba-dived where we could, and then rented full diving equipment from Tregelian so we could explore the deeper water. We saw plenty of wrecks, of course — this coast is notorious for them, but not a sign of the Spanish galleon.'

'And now Miranda has uncovered papers that can lead her to it?'

'That seemed to be what she was suggesting.'

'And you've come down to join her in

the hunt?' Kathryn asked, a dubious look on her face. 'Not sure you're built for scuba-diving no more, Professor.'

'Be right as rain when I get my new hip, but sadly that's not why we're here. I wish it were. No, a second letter arrived from Miranda. This time, all the envelope contained was a paper napkin with the words 'Help me' written on it in lipstick. I fear Miranda Catesby is in trouble.'

Luke and Kathryn exchanged glances.

'What is it?' the Prof asked.

'Miranda Catesby isn't most people's favourite person round here,' Kathryn said gently. 'She's upset a lot of people.'

'Really? How?'

'She's served Mum and a dozen other properties in the village with notices to quit. They have until the season's over to move out.'

'Miranda has asked you to leave Harbour Watch?' the Prof asked, astonished.

Kathryn nodded. 'And Bill Warren up at The Heights, Mr and Mrs Tregelly, the Penroses. Long-established Penrowan residents, every one.'

The Professor shook his head. 'That doesn't sound like Miranda at all. Like her father before her, Miranda has always been a champion of the Cornish residents of Penrowan. She could've sold all of those properties for a fortune to sec-ond-home owners or run them as holiday lets. Instead, she insisted on following her father's example and rented them at below-market rates to locals.'

Kathryn nodded. 'In many ways, Miranda Catesby has been a saviour to Penrowan. Without her generosity and community spirit, the village would've withered and died as so many have down here in the off-season. Instead, even in the depths of winter, we have a vibrant village full of life. Quite what will happen this autumn, however, I dread to think.'

'Has anyone spoken to Miranda?' the Professor asked.

'We've tried,' Luke said. 'When the notices to quit were first served, it took us all a few days to realise we weren't the only ones. In that time, practically everyone affected tried to contact her directly. We were told she'd gone away and that all communication had to be through her lawyers. Some London outfit. Not the locals she normally uses.'

'The Miranda I knew would never act this way.'

'If you ask me, it's her nephew, Teddy Catesby, who's pulling the strings,' Luke said disparagingly.

'Teddy is here in Penrowan?'

Kathryn and Luke nodded in unison. 'Showed up about two months ago, about as popular as a wasp at a picnic — about as friendly too,' Luke said.

'He's always been a rum sort of chap from what I hear,' the Professor said for Madison's benefit. 'Frittered away his inheritance from his father, Miranda's brother. Fancied himself as bit of an entrepreneur.'

'The man couldn't organise a booze-up in a brewery,' Luke said coldly. 'But he sure as hell knows how to cause trouble. None of us got anywhere with the lawyers. They just stonewalled us, saying there was no negotiation, no room for manoeuvre. First of October, Mum has to leave and hand over the keys.'

Madison glanced at Kathryn. She was staring out over the harbour, biting her lip. The woman was trying to be strong, but Madison could see the sheen of tears in her eyes. She noticed Luke reach for his mother's hand and give it a squeeze. She liked him very much at that moment.

'When we got no joy with the lawyers, me, Bill Warren and Mr Tregelly went up to Catesby Hall,' Luke said. 'Mary, the Catesby housekeeper, had told us Miranda was back. We were shown into the library by Mary, but we never saw Miranda. Instead, Teddy marched in. He was aggressive from the outset. 'You've been served with the papers,' he said. 'We've complied with the law. We need you to leave the properties on or before the date requested. Preferably before. Anyone outstays their welcome, I'll send the bailiffs in.' '

Madison saw Luke's free hand clench

into a fist. His other hand still lay protectively over his mother's.

'Outstay their welcome?' Luke repeated, his voice rising in indignation. 'How dare he? He may have been born at Catesby Hall with a silver spoon in his mouth, but I can count the number of years he's been in Cornwall since then on the fingers of one hand. If anyone has outstayed their welcome, it's him.'

'Miranda cannot be condoning this behaviour,' the Professor said.

'I wonder if she even knows?' Luke mused. 'Teddy said 'I'll send the bailiffs in,' not '*We'll* send them in.' '

'But the legal papers had Miranda's signature on them?'

Luke nodded.

'Mary says Miranda's ill,' Kathryn interjected. 'She's been away for treatment, some mystery ailment. Since she's got back, she's stayed in the east wing of the house, and Mary isn't allowed in there. All her meals are taken up to her by Teddy, but Mary says she's eating like a bird. Most of it comes back untouched.'

'How long has she been ill?' the Professor asked, concerned.

'A couple of months.'

The Professor rubbed his chin. 'So, she came down with this illness shortly after finding the Spanish galleon papers?'

Luke's eyes narrowed as he made the same connection as the Professor. They exchanged glances. Madison's gaze swung between them.

'I was right, then. Teddy Catesby is orchestrating the whole thing,' Luke said. 'But what do we do about it?'

'We need to speak to Miranda,' the Professor said firmly.

'Mary has been given her notice,' Kathryn said. 'She finishes next week. Teddy told her they don't want any outside help at the Hall anymore. His wife, Natasha, is going to look after the house.'

'We need to act as soon as possible then, and definitely before Mary leaves,' the Professor said decisively.

'Teddy and Natasha are dining at the Cliff Hotel tonight,' Kathryn said. 'It's their anniversary, apparently.'

'Brave decision, given the strength of local feeling,' the Professor commented.

'Natasha wanted to go somewhere fancy in London, so Mary told me. Teddy was having none of it. There's been a bit of trouble,' Kathryn admitted. 'Teddy's car was keyed in Tregelian last week, and I heard an egg was thrown at Teddy's back when he was walking down Fore Street in Penrowan on Monday. Apparently it's made him more determined to show himself locally, not less.'

'Lord of the manor,' Luke said bitterly.

'Both the Penrose girls serve up at the Cliff. They've already told the owners they'll refuse to serve them. I understand the owner is going to serve them himself. Only way they'll get a meal, so I heard.'

Madison finished her scone. Small towns were the same all over the world; everyone knowing everyone else's business. It was a blessing and a curse.

'I'll speak to Mary,' Luke said, standing as he checked his watch. 'She should still be helping at the bakery. I'll see if she can arrange to be at Catesby Hall tonight.

Hopefully she can let us in, or at the very least leave a door open.'

'Splendid idea,' the Professor agreed. 'You should go in through the tunnel. If my memory serves me right, it starts at the back of Bill Warren's property and comes out in the orchard.'

Luke nodded. 'I spent many a happy hour scrumping in that orchard when I was a boy.'

Madison raised her eyebrows. Somehow his nefarious past did not surprise her.

'That's settled then,' the Professor declared. 'We have a plan. Take Madison with you, Luke.'

He looked set to argue but then thought better of it and nodded.

'I only wish I could join you, but this old hip won't see me through that tunnel. You tell Miranda I'm here for her though. Bring her back with you, if you can.'

Luke nodded. 'We'll do our best, Professor.'

5

Madison Morley watched Luke Ryder shuffle on all fours ahead of her. She could not deny he had a cute backside clad in classic 501s; beaten up and frayed around the edges, the jeans were a bit like Ryder himself.

'Enjoying the view?' He twisted round.

Madison could see his left eyebrow arch in amusement in the wavering beam of her torch.

'In your dreams, Ryder!' she threw back.

He smirked and shuffled on.

'Is it my imagination, or can I smell the sea?' Madison asked.

Luke hitched round. 'We're coming up to the junction. Watch your head! It gets really low here, then widens out again.'

Madison watched as Luke lowered himself still further and slithered forward. Arching his back as though he were doing a yoga pose, he dragged himself into the opening beyond. Madison was astonished to see him then stand upright.

'Pass me your torch,' he said.

She did as he suggested. The tunnel was hewn from rock. Around her, water ran along channels worn into the surface over millennia. The overhang ahead was deep with a vicious-looking edge. She flattened herself as Luke had done and edged forwards, grateful she had worn black jeans and a black polo-neck sweater, even though Luke had teased her.

'Blimey!' he'd said as she had stepped into the hall of his mother's guest house. 'You look like every Hollywood film-maker's idea of a cat burglar. All that's missing is the rope and the ski mask.'

'I thought it would be practical,' she had rejoined, stung.

'On a warm spring evening?' That laconic eyebrow had risen in its now-familiar arch. 'Yeah, you don't look the least bit suspicious.'

He himself was wearing battered jeans, a white T-shirt advertising the fishermen's choir he purported to belong to, and an equally battered denim jacket. Madison was sorry, but there was no way she was taking sartorial advice from a man who thought it was a good idea to wear denim on denim, whatever the occasion.

She shrugged by him.

'At least let your hair down.'

She cried out as he seized her ponytail. 'Do you mind?' she said indignantly.

'Not at all.' He pulled the band free before running his fingers through her auburn hair and fanning it over her shoulders. 'Better,' he said, satisfied, and handed her the band. 'Put it back up before we go underground.'

She stuffed the band in her pocket. 'Jerk,' she muttered under her breath. How dare he?

Luke laughed. 'That's what the second Mrs Ryder called me when she left.'

'Really? What did the first Mrs Ryder call you?'

He grinned. 'She wasn't speaking to me at all by the time she left.' He held open the front door for Madison to walk through.

'Why doesn't that surprise me?'

He pulled the door shut and ran to catch her up. 'Are those designer togs?'

'J. Crew. Why?'

'You know they're going to get wet and dirty, right?' The smirk told her he was looking forward to it.

'Not a problem,' she said breezily.

Now Madison felt the overhang of rock brush her back.

'Careful! Don't try and come up too soon,' Luke warned.

'What are you doing?' she asked, alarmed as he squatted down and thrust his hand into the gap, brushing the small of her back as he did so.

'Giving you a little extra protection.'

She threw him a look. 'Your hand better not touch my backside, sunshine.'

'Afraid you might like it if it did?' His blue eyes danced in the beam of the torch.

'You have a very high opinion of yourself, don't you, Mr Ryder?' Madison wriggled free without further contact.

'I find if you don't value yourself highly, no one else does,' he rejoined.

She was going to hit back at him with the fact that she had a very low opinion of him herself, but the words died in her mouth as she swung the torch round in an arc. 'Wow!'

'It's quite something, isn't it?'

Madison nodded. The narrow tunnel of rock they had crawled through had opened out into a chamber tall enough for them to stand in and big enough to move around. To the left another tunnel, bigger and wider, led off into the darkness.

Madison tilted her head. 'I can't just smell the sea now — I can hear it, too.'

Luke nodded. 'The tunnel leads down to Holy Man Bay, and from there a path takes you up to Penrowan Church. The vicar still holds services on the beach to bless the fishermen on the Feast of St Elian in January. In autumn, when the storms roll in, the water sometimes makes it as far as that bend in the rock.'

'Couldn't we have come up that way?'

'Yeah, but it wouldn't have been as much fun.'

She was about to berate him when she

saw the tug of amusement at the side of his mouth.

'The tide is high. We would've had to secure the boat and wade in. The entrance isn't wide enough to drag the boat inside and up out of sight. It might've raised suspicions.'

She nodded. 'And that way?' She waved the torch in the opposite direction. The tunnel narrowed and dipped again, but not as much as the way they had come.

'That leads up to the house.' Luke's face was grim. 'Teddy Catesby and his goons can be an unpleasant bunch. Maybe you should stay here.'

'Not a chance, buster!'

Both tall, they had to walk at a stoop to avoid banging their heads on the roof of the tunnel.

'I guess people were smaller years ago,' Madison mused.

'Poor nutrition. You should see some of the doorways further up Pennycombe. I'd almost have to bend double to get in. Careful,' he warned, indicating a sudden hollow in the floor of the tunnel.

Madison negotiated it gracefully. There was a slight pull on her calf muscles, and although it was hard for her to get her bearings in the almost pitch dark, Madison had the sense they were moving uphill.

'We're about two hundred metres away from the orchard,' Luke said, his voice now an urgent whisper. 'The old rock that used to cover the entrance is probably still in place, overgrown by weeds now, but I wouldn't want to chance someone catching a glimpse of our torches. Best kill them, I think.'

Madison swallowed, apprehension swamping her. Without even the wavering beams of the torches to guide them, she genuinely wouldn't be able to see her own hand in front of her face.

As if sensing her unease, Luke turned and smiled. 'It's just a short walk from here. Tuck your fingers into the waistband of my jeans and I'll guide you through.'

Madison pulled a face. 'Or I could just hook my finger through one of the loops at the back of your jeans and hold on that way,' she said.

He smiled. 'Or you could do that,' he agreed.

She secured her finger through the loop of denim, feeling the leather of his belt beneath her finger.

'Okay?' he asked.

'Okay,' she confirmed, and licked her suddenly dry lips. Two hundred metres? They would be out in no time.

Luke extinguished his torch, and with the utmost reluctance, Madison followed suit. The darkness was extreme and instantly oppressive. She felt her heart rate soar. 'Why can't we see daylight yet?' she whispered.

'There's a kink in the tunnel up ahead. We should soon see daylight round the edge of the rock even if it's still in place. Donnee worry,' he assured her. 'We'll soon be outside again.'

Madison soothed herself with the idea of the warm spring-scented breeze fanning her face. Closing her eyes, she could almost feel it caressing her skin.

Not realising Luke had stopped, she ricocheted into his back. 'Why didn't you say you were stopping?' she cried indignantly.

'Shush!'

'Don't shush me!'

He turned, seizing her arm. 'Be quiet,' he said firmly. 'Someone is in the orchard.'

Luke edged forwards, taking Madison with him. Her heart was in overdrive now. What if the person in the orchard decided to enter the tunnel? How on earth were they going to explain themselves? She flirted with the idea of pretending to be a geologist studying the rock, but somehow she didn't think that bird was going to fly with whoever was out there.

As they neared the kink in the rock, the all-pervading darkness started to lift. Black became grey and then almost daylight. Madison unhooked her fingers from Luke's jeans.

He turned, gesturing to her to be quiet, and then took a step forward, chancing a look at the entrance to the tunnel. He quickly jerked his head back and returned to Madison's side. Placing his lips close to her ear, he whispered, 'The rock has been rolled aside. Someone other than us has been using the tunnel recently. It's all quiet out there now, but I'm going to take a look on my own. Stay here!'

Madison quickly nodded, giving her consent. As Luke moved away, she grabbed the edge of his jacket. 'Be careful,' she said, her nerves jangling.

He grinned. 'I'm always careful, love.'

She tried to count the minutes while he was gone, but it was hard to keep track because her mind kept wandering. Who would have thought, forty-eight hours ago, that she would be standing in an old Cornish smugglers' tunnel on her way to letting herself into the house of a woman she had never even met?

Seven minutes passed. Eight or was that nine? She decided once she had reached twelve she would edge her way quietly up to the entrance and risk a look. Twelve minutes came and went with no sign of Luke.

Taking a deep breath, she reached out to feel her way along the edge of the rocky wall. *Gently does it,* she told herself. When she reached the kink in the rock, she paused, her ears on high alert for the slightest sound. But all she could hear were the evening insects humming and clicking away and the breeze soughing through the overgrown grass. She dropped to a crouch and decided to continue.

The cooling breeze was refreshing; it beckoned her on. Madison could see long blades of grass waving at the entrance. She moved forwards with the stealth of a jaguar and hunkered down at the mouth of the tunnel.

The evening sunlight, although not directly in her eyes, was still dazzling after the darkness. With her eyes watering in response, it took her a moment or two to adjust her gaze. The orchard was full of gnarled apple trees, bent and twisted by the wind. For now though, they were wearing their best spring finery: delicate white and pink blossoms smothering the branches, weighing them down with their beauty.

Beyond the orchard, Madison could see an ancient brick and slate wall with an arched wooden gate, and through the gate, the edge of Catesby Hall itself. She scanned the orchard and saw Luke crouched behind an old shed. She was just about to gesture to him when he shook his head and pointed to his left before melting back behind what looked like a giant green roller.

She understood now why he hadn't returned. Something — or more likely someone — had cut him off. It was then that Madison heard the voices.

'We've searched the house, Mr Catesby. There's nothing there.'

'That's what my family thought for years, and then Miranda goes and finds that old chest. Check again.'

'But —'

'Check again. Then move on to the outbuildings.'

The voices were getting louder. Madison cursed silently. The blades of grass didn't look quite so full now that she might be forced to hide behind them, and there was no way she could back into the tunnel without alerting them to her presence, they were so damn close. Madison held her breath. She had to hope they changed direction.

'Did you organise the equipment to start searching the garden?'

'Yes, Mr Catesby. The team will be here with their equipment next week and they'll start a full survey.'

'Good. We must be thorough. If we don't turn up anything here, then we'll know the answer must be in one of the cottages in the village.'

'What about your aunt?'

'Miranda? What about her?'

'Are you sure she's told us everything?'

'She's a wily one, my aunt. I'd be amazed if she's told me everything, but I don't think even she knows the location of the galleon's treasure.'

Madison pressed herself to the rocky floor as a man appeared in her peripheral vision dressed in jeans and a T-shirt. He was a physical specimen, a bodybuilder type who clearly lifted a lot of weights.

He was closely followed by a second man, tall and slim, wearing tailored slacks and a linen jacket. That had to be Teddy Catesby. The first man must be his muscle, she guessed. Madison saw Catesby check his watch. She was close enough to see the sunlight glint on its gold band.

'Natasha and I need to leave. We're having dinner at the Cliff Hotel tonight.'

'Is that wise, Mr Catesby?' Muscles asked.

'Do you honestly think I'm going to let a bunch of yokels scare me away? The Catesbys have been on this land for over five hundred years. They need to know I cannot be intimidated.'

'Yes, boss.'

'Take the old smugglers' tunnel down to the village. It comes out at the back of Bill Warren's property. Head to the Smugglers' Inn; it's the one the locals use. Keep your ear to the ground and let me know what you find out.'

Madison thought her heart was going to burst right out of her chest. What were the chances of there being two smugglers' tunnels? Zilch. Muscles was turning, ready to head her way. She started to prepare an explanation. She could fall back on 'dumb tourist who happened to stumble into the tunnel from the beach'. Except that the tide was high! This was going to be a tough sell. It didn't help that Luke was right; she was dressed like a cat burglar.

Realising she was about to be discovered, she prepared to stand up. At least if she walked brazenly out into the garden, it would get them thinking; face down in the dirt only made her look more suspicious. She was just about to spring up when someone walked through the gate and into the orchard. Madison was astonished to see it was Luke.

'Catesby!' he yelled. 'I want a word with you.'

'What the hell ...?' Catesby turned in Luke's direction. 'You're on private property, Ryder.'

Luke marched a third of the way across the orchard and then stood with his hands on his hips. 'I'm not leaving until you come over here and talk to me.'

'Son of a ...' Catesby muttered under his breath. 'Come with me,' he said to Muscles. Striding purposefully, they moved quickly to the far side of the orchard.

Madison realised Luke had created the diversion in order to buy her time to get out of the tunnel. She looked left and right. The best place to hide was where she had first seen Luke behind the old shed and the giant green roller.

'What do you want, Ryder?'

'I want to talk to you about what you're doing to the villagers.'

'None of your business. You're not living in one of my properties.'

'My mother is.'

'Did you bring her with you?'

'Of course not.'

'Then as far as I am concerned, you have no authority to speak on her behalf, or anyone else's for that matter. Now, get off my land!'

'I don't need anyone else's authority to tell you that you're not welcome here.'

Luke was deliberately provoking the men to keep them looking his way, Madison realised. Crouching, she set off at a run for the cover of the shed. She guessed Luke was watching her progress because he ratcheted up the tension by moving menacingly towards Catesby as she began her run.

'Get your hands off me, Ryder!'

'Step back, Mr Ryder!' Muscles warned.

'You're still the same snivelling little spoilt brat who skinned his knees on the rocks in Holy Man Bay,' Luke said. 'You think you can bully everyone? Well, you can't bully me.'

Madison made it to the sanctuary of the shed, her heart almost popping out of her chest, not so much from the effort but the fear of discovery. Panting for breath, she chanced a look.

'Hit him,' Catesby said.

'Sir?'

'You heard me. He's trespassing on private property and he's just assaulted me. Now, hit him.'

Madison cringed as Muscles aimed a fist at Luke's face. For a tall man, Luke was fast, but not fast enough, and the blow landed on the side of his face.

'Now eject him from my property. Better yet, drive him back to Penrowan station and leave him there. I catch you up here again, Ryder, I'll call the police and press charges. Won't that make your mother proud?'

Madison watched Luke struggle against Muscles' iron grip. 'That's so typical of you, Catesby. You get someone else to do your dirty work.'

She saw Luke glance in her direction and give an almost imperceptible nod as he was led away.

Catesby brushed down his jacket. 'Why have a dog and bark yourself?' Catesby mused. As he drew level with the old wooden gate, he paused and looked back at the entrance to the tunnel before scanning the orchard. Madison melted back behind the shed and held her breath. Then she heard the sound of the wooden gate being pulled home.

Within moments of their departure, she was aware once more of the breeze through the trees and the industrious insects. She'd lost her wingman. What now? If Muscles was driving Luke back to the station, it would take him a while to come back up to the property. *I guess you're on your own, kiddo.*

6

Madison gave it twenty minutes before she moved. Being able to check her watch this time made measuring the timescale easy. Maintaining her patience and composure, however, was a whole lot more difficult, but she knew she had to give Teddy Catesby and his wife a chance to depart for their meal at the Cliff Hotel.

When she deemed it safe to move, Madison sprinted across the orchard and nudged open the gate in the garden wall. In front of her was a sheltered kitchen garden, the beds surrounded by neat box hedging, and ahead lay Catesby Hall.

It was a substantial red brick building. Madison could see the kitchen door. Mary had promised Luke that she would leave the kitchen window open with the back door key within easy reach. She'd also said there were always at least two security men in the house at any one time.

Madison sidled up to the window and took a quick look into the kitchen. The room was empty and she could see the key on the windowsill. She offered up a silent thank-you to the unknown Mary. Stretching her fingers through the narrow gap, Madison clasped the key. As her fingers closed around it, she heard voices. Withdrawing the key, she sank down, pressing herself against the brickwork.

The tap exploded into life on the other side of the wall, making Madison jump. It sounded like a waterfall. She strained her ears. Two men by the sound of it, exchanging mocking insults about a football match, an Englishman and a Scot. A boiling kettle drowned out their speech. She heard the kettle click off, followed by the rattle of spoons against china.

'We should check the gardens,' the English one said.

His companion swore. 'Boss is away for the evening. Let's just grab some R&R while we can.'

Madison looked around her. It was long sprint to the side of the house, about as long again back to the walled orchard. She started to pray the English one would abandon his check of the garden for just one evening.

'Besides, kickoff's in ten minutes.'

The Scot had obviously won the day. She listened to their footsteps recede and from somewhere inside the cavernous house, a television roared into life. That would make things easier.

Madison quickly opened the back door and pulled it to behind her. Mary had said Miranda Catesby was in the east wing, almost directly at the opposite end of the house from the main kitchen. The east wing was served by a little kitchenette on the ground floor, but Teddy Catesby had made it quite plain that Mary was not to go into the east wing at all. That was before he dispensed with her services altogether, of course.

Pleased she'd worn her Converse trainers, Madison stood in the parquet-floored hallway and took a moment to get her

bearings. The sound of the blaring television was coming from another small
hallway. She sprinted past it undetected
and made her way across the ground floor
of the house, following the route Luke
had briefly outlined as they had set out
that evening. Thank goodness she had
been paying attention.

She recognised the ornately carved
heavy oak door that Luke had said
marked the entrance to the east wing.
There was an elaborate wrought-iron key
in the lock. Madison turned it and let
herself inside. She was greeted by a flight
of steep oak stairs. She ran up them at
a jog, her ponytail bouncing against her
neck. Once on the landing, she was faced
with a corridor and a number of doors
leading from it on either side. Only one
had a key in the lock, she noticed — the
one at the far end.

Madison turned the key and opened
the door. The room was large and filled
with lots of dark, heavy furniture. There
were leaded glass windows on two sides.
She caught a glimpse of a gravel drive

and a fountain. She had not only moved from one side of the house to the other, but also from the back to the front.

The curtain hangings were dark silk brocade. The floor was made up of dark wooden planks. The walls, too, were wood-panelled. With twilight descending, it had the effect of draining all the light from the room. It was leaching away even as Madison stood there. She could make out the shape of a wardrobe, a large chest of drawers and against the wall an enormous four-poster bed, but the outline of the furniture was already starting to blend into the dark walls and floor.

She reached to pluck the torch from her belt, but it was missing. She must have dropped it as she ran from the tunnel. A little unnerved by the semi-darkness, she edged further into the room. At first glance, she had thought the four-poster bed was empty. Now she realised there was a woman there, hunkered down under the covers. Her eyes were tightly shut, her breathing regular. Miranda Catesby?

Madison had a moment's doubt. While Luke had been diligent in explaining the route to her, he had neglected to give her one vital piece of information: a description of what Miranda Catesby actually looked like. Dare she wake the woman and risk a scene? Madison's heart thudded. *Wait!* She told herself. *Think about it. You had to get through two locked doors to get here. This has to be Miranda Catesby.*

Madison went down on her knees beside the bed, knowing that to wake someone and then loom over them would be even more frightening. She touched the woman's shoulder gently. 'Miranda?'

The woman's eyes opened instantly. Madison almost toppled backwards from the shock. Vivid blue discs widened as they stared at her.

'Who are you?' The voice was firm, commanding. Not at all what Madison had expected.

'I'm Compton Morley's granddaughter, Madison.'

At the mention of her grandfather's

name, the change in the woman's demeanour was instant. She sat up, and although her hand went quickly to her head, she nevertheless pushed the covers back with her other hand and swung her legs free.

'I knew he'd come. Is he here?' Miranda looked around her.

'No, he's waiting for us in the village.'

Miranda nodded. 'Get me some clothes. There are trousers and a jumper in the wardrobe.'

Madison did as she was asked. Miranda had already stripped off her nightgown and had tugged on her underwear when Madison returned to the bed with the clothes. 'He got my cry for help?'

'Yes.'

'Teddy slipped up, allowed Mary to bring one of my meals. I begged her to send my note to Compton. But I haven't seen her since, so I had no way of knowing if she did it or not. Where are Teddy and Tash and the gorillas?'

'Teddy and his wife are having dinner

at the Cliff Hotel tonight,' Madison told her. 'One of their men is driving Luke Ryder back to the village, and the other two are watching football downstairs.'

'What's Luke got to do with this?' Miranda asked sharply.

'He came with me tonight. He had to create a diversion so I could get out of the smugglers' tunnel without Teddy and one of his men seeing me.'

'Luke's a good man,' said Miranda, pulling on a pair of trainers. She stood, swaying slightly as she did so. Madison held out her arm and Miranda grasped it. 'They've kept me sedated and cooped up in here for weeks. I've always hated this bloody room. I haven't had much to eat, so you'll have to forgive me — I'm a little light-headed.'

'Don't worry,' Madison said automatically, although her mind was already turning to the steep stairs they would have to descend to exit the east wing. And then what? There had been a carefully laid plan to get into the house, but she and Luke had hardly discussed what would happen once they were there. 'We'll just wing it,' he'd said cheerfully.

'Do you have a car?' Madison asked hopefully.

Miranda gave her a sharp look. 'Several, but we'll never get into the garages and start a car without Teddy's men hearing us.'

Madison nodded. Besides which, Muscles must have delivered Luke back to Penrowan railway station some time ago and be on his way back to the house by now. Almost as the thought formed in her mind, headlights bounced through the room, moving across the wall.

'Teddy and Tash?' Miranda asked.

Madison picked up on the black note of fear in her voice. 'Muscles probably,' Madison replied. 'Back from dropping Luke in the village.'

'Muscles?' Miranda smiled. 'An apt nickname. We'd better not waste any time. These boys are all ex-military. They work to a pattern. Muscles, as you call him, will park his car and then check in with his mates before coming up here and checking on me.'

Madison watched as Miranda formed three pillows into the form of a body in the bed, using a heavy vase to make a dent in the top pillow before pulling the covers up to cover the neck of the vase. She stood back, admiring her handiwork. 'That should do it.'

'I'll pull the drapes,' Madison said.

'Good idea! But be quick. We don't have much time.'

Madison dragged the heavy material along. The gloom was now complete. She bumped her knee on the edge of the bed and stifled a cry. Then she felt Miranda's warm hand in hers. 'Follow me!' the woman declared. Madison complied gratefully, wondering which one of them was doing the rescuing.

Madison turned the key in the lock of Miranda's bedroom door and the two women ran down the corridor. They took the steep stairs one step at a time, Miranda holding tightly to the handrail with one hand and Madison's arm with the other. Because the stairs were too narrow for them to walk down two abreast, it was an awkward and time-consuming manoeuvre, but at last they made it to the corridor, Madison's heart thumping against her ribcage with every step. It was with a huge sense of relief that she turned the key in the door leading to the east wing.

They both heard the approaching footsteps at the same time. Miranda quickly pulled Madison into a side room and the two women huddled behind the door, straining every sinew to listen to what was going on outside. They heard the key turn in the lock of the east wing door and the sound of Muscles taking the stairs two at a time.

'He'll just look into my room,' Miranda said confidently. 'They won't realise I'm gone until the morning, unless Teddy decides to check on his return, but we'll be long gone by then.'

Madison wished she shared Miranda's confidence. A couple of minutes passed before they heard Muscles close the east wing door and lock it once more. The pillows and vase had clearly done the trick. He wasn't going to be raising the alarm any time soon.

'What now?' Miranda asked.

Madison was nonplussed. 'I —'

'You got here via the smugglers' tunnel, didn't you?' Madison nodded. 'Then that's the way we'll leave. I'm sure Bill Warren won't mind if we suddenly pop up at the back of his garden.' Miranda made her way over to the French doors on the far side of the room.

'The tunnel is very tight in places. Are you sure you'll be okay?' Madison knew she had said the wrong thing as soon as the words were out of her mouth.

Miranda Catesby's nostrils flared, and there was a hint of steel in her voice when she spoke. 'I'll be fine.'

Madison still had her doubts, despite Miranda's bravado. The tunnel hadn't been easy for her to negotiate, and she hadn't been kept a prisoner within her own home with little food or fresh air. The older woman was clearly running on adrenaline, but what happened when that ran out? Alarmed at the prospect, Madison said, 'It's pitch black in one section, and I dropped my torch.'

'I've been walking that tunnel since I was barely five years old. I could do it with my eyes closed. Don't worry.'

Putting aside her misgivings, Madison nodded and followed Miranda to the French doors. 'These doors open onto the terrace at the side of the property,' Miranda explained. 'From there we can cross to the orchard without anyone seeing us.'

Madison nodded. Miranda set off like a gazelle across the grounds, catching Madison completely unaware. It was hard to imagine how anyone had ever managed to contain, let alone cage, this resourceful and agile woman. That Teddy Catesby had been able to do such a thing made him a formidable opponent in Madison's eyes.

It took just a few minutes to reach the entrance to the smugglers' tunnel. Both women went a little way inside before pausing to catch their breath, lest they be spotted at this late stage.

'Ready?' Miranda asked.

With a grim look of determination on her face, Madison nodded, screwing up her courage, ready to face the blackness once more. Before she did so, however, she saw the beam of a torch bounce across the opposite wall of the tunnel, and both women automatically shrank back.

'Miranda, is that you?' A rich, deep voice reverberated from the depths of the tunnel.

The two women exchanged glances. 'Luke?' they cried in unison.

The beam of the torch jerked up and down and they heard the sound of running feet. 'Ladies! Nice evening for a walk,' he said jovially. 'It's good to see you, Miranda. You had us worried.'

'I had myself worried, lad,' she admitted.

'Are you okay?' he asked, scanning her face.

'Don't you start!' she admonished him. 'I think Madison is half-afraid I'm going to konk out on her. I'm sure I can make it to Bill Warren's.'

'No need,' Luke said. 'I thought we might need a quick getaway. *Kathryn's Pride* is waiting for us.'

'I thought you were worried about someone seeing the boat, which is why we didn't come that way?' Madison asked.

'I was, but it seemed like the lesser of two evils once we got separated.' She nodded. 'Are you okay?' he asked.

'I'm fine,' Madison said. It was on the tip of her tongue to say, 'Better for seeing you,' but she just couldn't manage to get the words out. Luke Ryder seemed pretty sure of himself already. She could imagine it would not take much encouragement to make him utterly insufferable.

The tunnel didn't seem as scary or as long on the return journey. It helped that Luke's torch was burning brightly, showing them the way, and that no one was pursuing them. It didn't stop Madison from casting a nervous look over her shoulder now and then, but there was no sign of anyone behind them.

Only a tiny spit of sand was visible when they arrived at Holy Man Bay, and the tide was beginning to encroach even on that, Madison was disconcerted to discover. In front of them a wooden boat bounced on the high water, nudging and bumping the rocks, but Luke's knot around an old iron ring had held firm.

'We'll need to climb out onto the rocks and then down into the boat,' he explained. 'I'll go first so I can steady the boat as you both climb in. Be careful — the rocks are slippery; I nearly went in the drink on the way in. Do you want to take my arm, Miranda?'

Miranda shook her head. 'Better we each make our own way across, I think.'

They watched as Luke scrambled over the rocks and dropped into the boat. It pitched under his weight. He grinned at them and motioned for Miranda to join him.

As with the sprint across the garden, Madison was surprised by Miranda's strength and agility. The frankly frail woman she had first encountered seemed to be receding with every step they took away from her impromptu prison. She watched Miranda scamper across the rocks. She had taken Luke's outstretched hand in no time.

Madison took a deep breath. The youngest of the three, she knew she couldn't be seen to be letting the side down. It was a matter of pride. She pulled herself up onto the first rock. Its surface was slick, but her trainers gained enough purchase to propel her onto the next. She was one rock away from joining her companions when Luke called out a warning.

'Big wave coming in, Maddy. Crouch down so that your centre of gravity is lower, and spread your arms out.'

Madison did as he suggested. The large wave sent the boat into a frenzied dance before rolling on and slapping against the rocks. It topped the rock Madison stood on, and cold seawater drenched her shoes and socks. The splash and pull of the water might have been enough to send her off balance if she'd been standing.

She gave Luke a grateful smile. 'Thank you.'

'You're welcome.' He returned the smile.

She stood a little gingerly and made her way onto the last rock before grabbing hold of Luke's hand and easing herself into the boat, relieved to be aboard.

Luke quickly released the rope before the outboard motor roared into life, the smell of diesel filling the air. Expertly guiding the little boat away from the rocks, he masterfully took account of the massive swell and pull of the high tide. Madison was impressed. Only someone who had been sailing these waters all their life could have managed it.

He quickly manoeuvred the boat alongside *Kathryn's Pride*, and they all climbed aboard before he secured a line so that the wooden boat was pulled along in its wake. 'Let's go home,' he said as he gunned the engine.

He turned the boat towards the headland to their left. Madison knew that hidden beyond it in the steep fold of the hills was Penrowan. Spots of rain started to fall from the dark sky. She settled her arm around Miranda's shoulders. 'Okay?' she asked.

Miranda nodded, a smile on her face. 'I am now.'

As they bounced across the water, Madison could see a faint smudge on the horizon, heralding the impending darkness. The gloom was made all the more apparent by the bright lights burning ashore. Madison thought of Rock Cottage. They would soon be ensconced within its thick walls, sheltered from the night, safe from Teddy Catesby and his men.

Madison turned her head to study Luke in the torchlight. He was standing tall and strong at the back of the boat, steering them home with the lightest of touches on the controls. His hair was being blown back by the headwind they were sailing into, but he seemed happy despite the cold rain spattering them all. She thought she even caught him humming quietly to himself when the wind abated a little.

He was a man at home in the elements, she realised. Not someone to be cooped up in an office all day; the complete opposite to Will. It took her a moment to recognise the flutter of attraction in her stomach. Astonished that her body could react like that without any direct input from her conscious self, Madison made herself remember the phone rock incident and what an idiot he had allowed her to make of herself. That quelled her feelings.

She turned back into the headwind to find Miranda watching her as she looked at Luke. There was a knowing smile on the older lady's face. Madison wanted to shake her head and say, 'Oh no! It's not what you think.' But the words would have been ripped away by the wind, and Miranda was already turning round, eager for her first glimpse of Penrowan Harbour.

The harbour was a magical sight even in such challenging conditions, perhaps especially so. The lights of the cottages on either side of the village and along the cleft of the valley floor blazed brightly.

From her vantage point out at sea, Madison thought it looked as though a giant had thrown handfuls of stars into the air and they had come to rest in a chaotic jumble over the hillsides of Penrowan.

'Beautiful, isn't it?' Luke said, looking down at her.

Madison nodded. 'It's really something,' she agreed.

He lowered their speed and skimmed the outer harbour wall, then skilfully turned to negotiate the inner harbour. It took Madison a moment to get her bearings, and then she recognised Rock Cottage, so different when viewed from the harbour itself. It rose, majestic, dozens of coloured fairy lights strung along the balustrade of the decking. As she looked closer, she could see her grandfather and Kathryn waiting on the decking, taking no heed of the rain that was now lashing down.

'Home sweet home,' Luke declared as he brought the boat up to his mooring beneath the cottage. He tossed the rope up. Kathryn caught it deftly and secured it. 'The steps will be wet, so hold tight,' he said.

Miranda sprang up, rejuvenated from the exhilarating boat ride, and climbed the ladder without hesitation. Madison noted how Luke covered the bottom of the ladder, ready to catch her if she fell, or at least soften her landing. There it was again, darn it — that feeling in her stomach.

Her grandfather and Kathryn helped Miranda up onto the decking, and her grandfather quickly enveloped Miranda in a bear hug. The babble of excited conversation floated down to Madison, though she was too distant to hear what was being said over the loud slap of the water against the boat.

She gripped the ladder and began to climb. Luke was several rungs behind. To her acute embarrassment, her foot slipped on a piece of seaweed that had wrapped itself around the ladder. She felt her heel impact somewhere on Luke's body. 'Sorry!' she cried.

'I rescue you and I get a kick in the shoulder for my trouble,' he grumbled.

'I said I was sorry. And anyway, I think 'rescue' is a pretty broad interpretation of what just happened. Miranda and I would have found our way back.'

Luke grinned. 'You still looked pretty relieved to see me when I showed up, Maddy. Admit it — you were pleased I was there,' he said.

The grin was infuriating. Now she remembered why she had been able to overlook his athletic build and handsome face so successfully up until now, because whenever he opened his mouth, something annoying came out of it.

She hauled herself onto the deck. Her grandfather, Kathryn and Miranda had disappeared inside. She took a step towards the double doors.

Luke was quickly beside her, flipping the catch and opening the door. 'I'll take your silence as a yes,' he said, slipping into the kitchen ahead of her.

A retort formed on her tongue but she let it go. If she was truthful with herself, she *had* been glad to see him. The prospect of weaving their way through the tunnel had not been an appealing one. Despite Miranda's assurances, she had been worried about the woman, and the thought of squeezing through the lowest overhang of rock had been particularly playing on her mind. Luke's appearance, and the fact they could leave via the larger tunnel which led to the sea, had been more than welcome. She smiled ruefully. Admitting that to herself was tough enough, but admitting it to Luke Ryder? That was unthinkable.

7

Madison and Kathryn returned to Rock Cottage early the next day. 'Mackerel sky,' Kathryn said, pointing to the watery sun.

'Mackerel?' Madison queried.

'The clouds look like the skin of a mackerel,' Kathryn explained. 'Mackerel sky and mare's tails make tall ships carry low sails. Rain's coming.'

More rain? No wonder Cornwall was so lush and green.

After their rescue of Miranda, they had enjoyed a restorative cup of tea, and then Kathryn had bundled Miranda into one of the spare bedrooms, insisting that she needed to rest, which seemed ironic given that she appeared to have spent so much time confined to bed the last few weeks. However, Madison could see that after the exhilaration of the flight from Catesby Hall, Miranda was starting to fade, her energy levels visibly dipping as her eyelids drooped.

Now, they found the Professor and Luke in the kitchen drinking mugs of tea. 'The Doc's with Miranda,' Luke explained as he splashed tea into two more mugs.

The blow Luke had taken from Muscles was clear to see in the morning light. There was a slight rise to his left cheekbone and a vivid, angry bruise.

Kathryn stroked her son's face. 'You should press charges,' she said, pursing her lips.

'He'd press them right back. Trespass. Assault. Besides, if I hadn't taken a smack in the face, Madison would have been discovered, so it was worth it.' He grinned at her. 'Any time you feel like saying thank you...' He left the sentence hanging.

Madison could feel the weight of her grandfather's stare, and Kathryn's too. 'Thank you,' she said quietly.

Luke's grin widened. 'I've had worse,' he admitted. That, she could believe.

'I owe you, my boy,' the Professor said.

Why couldn't Luke be just a little bit gracious? Why did he have to fish for compliments? If only he were a little more modest, Madison might have felt able to be fulsome in her praise, instead of being nudged into it. Possibly.

They turned as the Doc came downstairs. 'Miranda tells me she's been locked in for many weeks. It's clear she started to lose track of time during her incarceration. She's not had enough to eat or drink. From what I can gather, they gave her the barest minimum.'

The Professor swore under his breath.

'We'll soon put that right,' Kathryn said with forced jollity, but Madison could see the anger in her eyes.

'Easy does it,' the Doc warned. 'Small portions. Little and often. Gradually increase the amounts over the next few weeks. If you give her too much too soon, her body won't be able to handle the extreme change.'

Kathryn nodded.

'I'm going to run some blood tests. Miranda seems perfectly lucid, but she was sedated for part of her imprisonment. She thinks they were standard sleeping pills, but I want to make sure there are no lasting effects. In my opinion, we should be telling the police, but Miranda is adamant she doesn't want them brought in at this stage.'

'A prison cell is too good for Teddy Catesby,' Luke said.

'She says she'll regain her strength here and then tackle her nephew herself,' the Doc continued. 'Only then will she contact the police and bring charges. I have to say, that doesn't sit well with me, but as I've known Miranda all my life, so I will honour her wish. However...' The Doc raised his finger in warning. 'Miranda is not to be left alone. While she is still weak and vulnerable, Teddy may try to snatch her back. I have no doubt that this time he wouldn't hold her at Catesby Hall, and if he spirited her away I think there's a very good chance we'd never see her again. If she goes missing, I'll go straight to the police.'

Everyone nodded.

'I'll be in touch in a couple of days when I have the blood test results. I'll handle them myself so no one at the surgery knows I've seen her.'

'Thank you, Doc.' Luke showed him out.

Kathryn had thoughtfully provided some clothes for Miranda, which she took upstairs. A few minutes later they descended together. Miranda sank gratefully into one of the squashy armchairs near the fireplace. The Professor took the armchair opposite hers.

'I'll do you a spot of breakfast.' Kathryn caught Luke's look. 'Pigeon portions to start off,' she said.

She bustled off, leaving Miranda, the Professor, Luke and Madison behind. Madison sat at one end of the sofa, Luke at the other. She knew they each had so many questions, but no one wanted to start, worried about bombarding Miranda, who looked tired and drained.

Miranda looked at each of them in turn. 'I owe all of you a huge thank-you. Kathryn too,' she said calmly.

They all quickly demurred, but Miranda held up her hand. 'Now is not the time for false modesty.' Her voice was strong even though she looked fragile. 'I have no doubt that when Teddy had no more use for me, he would've finished me off.'

Madison was shocked as much by the matter-of-fact way Miranda spoke as by the words themselves.

'Teddy will have no reason to look for me here, so for the time being I'm safe. If I may impose upon you for a little longer, Luke...'

'Of course.'

'It will give me a chance to get my strength back, and then we must take the fight to him.'

Luke shook his head, his hands curling into fists. 'I've always known Teddy was a bad apple, but this...'

'It's amazing what the lure of treasure will do,' Miranda said quietly.

'All of this is because of the Spanish galleon?' Luke asked, astonished. 'The galleon is a myth, a Penrowan fairytale.'

'No, Luke,' Miranda said softly. 'The galleon is real, and so is the treasure she's guarding.'

'Do you know where it is?' the Professor asked eagerly, leaning forwards.

'Sadly, no, but I know a lot more than my nephew. I'm not sure if the Professor has filled you two young people in on the rosewood chest of papers I found ...' Miranda raised an enquiring eyebrow.

The Professor nodded. 'I told Madison before we left London, and I told Luke about it before he went to Catesby Hall last night. What was in the chest, Miranda? More of Milton Catesby's journals?'

'No, something far more enlightening,' Miranda said. She, too, was now leaning forwards, her eyes clear and alert. 'Bricked up in the priest hole were papers belonging to Cornelius Catesby. He was the owner of Catesby Hall at the time the galleon was wrecked.'

'What did they say?' the Professor enquired, trying valiantly to keep the eagerness from his tone, but failing.

'Cornelius wrote about a succession of storms that lashed the coast over three consecutive nights in the November of 1567. Several ships were lost, and on the last night, the Spanish galleon was driven onto the rocks in Holy Man Bay. Most of the sailors were lost as the ship was torn to shreds, but a handful made it ashore, one of whom was Javier Diaz.

'Cornelius found Diaz unconscious in the mouth of the smugglers' tunnel. He carried him back to the Hall and tended to his wounds. When he came to, Diaz told Cornelius that the galleon was part of the treasure fleets. These fleets sailed from Spain with goods for the Spanish colonies in South America, and on the return voyage they carried treasure from the New World back to their Spanish homeland.

'Diaz said even though the fleets were guarded and sailing in convoy, they were attacked by privateers sponsored by the English government, and the convoy was broken up. A series of storms then hit, and the galleon lost contact with all the other vessels. Bound for Seville, it ended up wildly off course and found itself in Cornish waters.

'As the raging wind drove the ship on, Diaz was ordered by the captain to attend him in his cabin. The captain instructed Diaz and three other men to take five rosewood chests from his cabin and link them all by rope to one another, then cast them overboard at the last possible moment before the ship was lost.

'Diaz said that the men did as they were told. The chests were extremely heavy and it was hard work, but they accomplished their task; and as the ship ran aground, they sent the chests over the seaward side of the ship. The chests sank without trace, and Diaz and the other men dived into the water, desperate to save themselves.

'Cornelius asked Diaz if he knew what was in the chests. Diaz beckoned Cornelius closer and said he was sure the chests contained eight-real pieces — silver coins, also known as Spanish dollars. It's where the term 'pieces of eight' comes from,' Miranda said.

They all looked up as Kathryn entered carrying a tray. 'I've made you a poached egg on toast and a little bacon,' she said. 'There's some fresh orange juice there, too.'

Miranda accepted the tray onto her lap with a warm smile. 'Thank you, Kathryn.'

Kathryn looked at the others. 'You needn't think Miranda is going to carry on talking while she's eating,' she said sternly. 'Hardly likely to aid the digestion, is it? I doubt the poor lady wants to be gawped at while she's eating, either, so you can all come along into the kitchen and give the lady some peace.'

One after the other they went into the kitchen, Kathryn following on behind before firmly shutting the door. 'Spanish galleons and pieces of eight,' she tutted. 'Whatever next? A one-legged man and a bloody parrot, I suppose?'

'Hard to believe, Kathryn, I know,' the Professor said, 'but Miranda appears to have found an account of the wreck that is contemporaneous to the event itself. The only thing we had to go on years ago were the vague ramblings of Milton Catesby in his journals some three hundred years later, no doubt pulled together by half-truths, vague remembrances, and probably a good dash of embellishment.'

Lost in thought, the group lapsed into silence as several minutes passed.

'The chests must have been recovered, though,' Luke mused. 'You said yourself, Professor, that you and Miranda scoured every inch of Holy Man Bay. Hundreds of divers have explored that area and the myriad wrecks along the shoreline. I've done it myself. There's no way the chests are still down there.'

'They're not.' They turned to find Miranda standing in the doorway holding her tray, upon which were an empty plate and glass. 'That was delicious, Kathryn. Thank you.'

Kathryn took the tray from her, and Miranda pulled back a chair and joined the others at the kitchen table, where she continued her narrative. 'Urged on by Diaz,' she said, 'Cornelius returned to the bay in search of the chests. Men from Penrowan were scavenging amongst the wreckage, carrying away anything of value that could be usefully salvaged. Cornelius reckoned that the weight of the chests would've carried them down to the bottom of the bay; but, taking his bearings from where the remains of the ship had washed up, he calculated there was a chance the chests might've landed on the edge of the shelf.' She turned to Madison. 'The shelf is a spit of land that protrudes from the shoreline about eight hundred metres and then drops away dramatically.'

'But this was the 1500s,' Madison said. 'There was no diving equipment. Even if the chests had landed on this spit of land, how could they ever be recovered?'

'By exercising patience, my dear,' the Professor interjected.

'I don't understand.'

'He waited until the following spring and the vernal equinox!' Luke exclaimed. 'Wow, that's clever.' He turned to Madison. 'At every full moon and every new moon, high tides are highest and low tides are lowest. They're known as spring tides, although it's got nothing to do with the season. Twice a year at the autumnal and vernal equinoxes, the spring tides are the highest and lowest of all. The Spanish galleon ran aground in November, too late for the autumnal equinox, so Cornelius had to wait until the vernal equinox in the spring of the following year before he could put his theory into practice. The tide would have swept right out. Not so far as to reveal the edge of the shelf, but far enough that you could comfortably swim down and investigate it.'

'So he waited all those months?' Madison asked. Miranda nodded.

Luke whistled. 'Imagine how frustrating it must have been, thinking there was a small fortune in silver coins down there and having to wait for the conditions to be right to recover it. He did recover it though, didn't he?'

'Yes,' Miranda answered. 'He recorded it all in his journal. How Javier spent the intervening months getting his strength back and working on a detailed painting of the Spanish galleon in full sail, while Cornelius practised holding his breath, increasing the time by a few seconds every day, training for the day of the recovery.'

'Remarkable,' the Professor said.

'When the vernal equinox arrived, Cornelius and Javier were waiting. They had the whole bay to themselves. They found the chests tied together just as Javier had described. Together they were able to sever the rope and bring the chests back to shore one by one. Once they had them safely inside the smugglers' tunnel, they opened them. Cornelius said he'd never seen so much silver: there were three chests full of eight-real pieces, just as Javier had surmised, and two chests with gold plate and candlesticks.'

'What happened next?' Madison asked, caught up in the tale.

'Cornelius and Javier split the hoard between them. Now that he was fit and strong, Javier was keen to see his homeland again. He went to London and found passage on a ship. He wrote to Cornelius a few months later to say he was a healthy and happy man living in his home village with his family around him.'

'And what of Cornelius?' the Professor asked.

'The Catesby family are Roman Catholics — lapsed on my part, I fear. But in 1569, Cornelius Catesby was part of the Rising of the North. At that time, the Catesby family had land and property in Yorkshire as well as Cornwall. Cornelius and the other Catholics wanted to put Mary, Queen of Scots on the throne of England, and Cornelius used part of the treasure to help fund the uprising. The rest he hid. Unfortunately, the northern rebellion failed, and Cornelius fled first to Scotland and then to France.'

'What happened to him?' Madison asked.

'He caught a chill on the voyage and died shortly after arriving. He never saw Cornwall again. The Hall passed to his younger brother, my many-times great-grandfather, who'd renounced his

Catholic faith, in public at least, and agreed to toe the Protestant line.

'Cornelius knew the uprising was risky and likely to fail. He signed off in his journal the day before he joined the gathering forces in the north, saying that he was going to seal his papers inside the priest hole and recover them when he came home. But in case he didn't make it back, he left the following instruction: 'Should I not return and you should chance upon my journal, seek out the Spanish galleon, and behind it you will discover riches beyond your wildest dreams.' '

The group sat in silence for a moment.

Luke threw Miranda a sceptical look. 'How do we know Cornelius didn't just spend all the money?' he asked.

Miranda shook her head. 'We don't, but it doesn't seem likely. The last entry read: 'NW six paces, EW three paces'.'

Kathryn tsked. 'Pieces of eight, six paces here and three paces there. You've all taken leave of your senses!' she declared.

'How much of this does your nephew

know?' the Professor asked.

'When I realised Teddy was sniffing about, I ripped out the last page of Cornelius's journal. Teddy knows that the treasure is hidden, but that's all. He and his men are wildly knocking holes in the walls and the ceilings at the Hall. They plan to start on the garden and the outbuildings next. They're using a sledgehammer to crack a nut. Of course, they may get lucky and stumble on the treasure, but what they should really be looking for is the Spanish galleon.'

'Javier's painting?' the Professor said.

'I'm sure of it,' Miranda agreed. 'I believe his painting either marks the spot where the treasure is hidden or contains some clue that could lead us to it. I'd just completed my search of Catesby Hall when Teddy arrived, got wind of what I was up to, and refused to leave. He, however, assumed I was searching for the treasure itself, not a painting of the ship. I decided not to disabuse him of this notion,' Miranda added, a twinkle in her eye.

'The painting is over five hundred years old. The likelihood of it still surviving is remote,' the Professor mused. 'Not impossible, but remote.'

'You know my family never threw anything away, Compton,' Miranda said. 'Centuries of stuff has accumulated in dusty corners, and when they started to run out of space at the Hall they simply shipped things out to the houses in the village and stored them there in the attics.'

Luke and Kathryn exchanged glances. 'Is that why you've served me with a notice to quit?' Kathryn asked sullenly.

'A notice to quit?' Miranda repeated.

'Yes. I've got until October to pack up and move out.'

'I haven't served you with a ...' She stopped. 'Teddy must have forged my signature. Kathryn, I am so sorry. I will put this right, I promise. I won't see you leave Harbour Watch. It's your home.'

'And the others?' Kathryn asked.

'There are others?' Miranda asked, horrified.

Luke told her about the rest of the

villagers who had been given notice to leave. Miranda passed a hand over her eyes with a heavy sigh. 'I *will* put this right. For everyone,' she declared. 'Without the locals living in Penrowan year round, the community will only come to life in the summer months. We can't have that. We won't.' She brought her fist down on the kitchen table, making the china rattle. 'I must speak to my lawyer.' Agitated, she stood up. 'I must get him to undo all the damage Teddy has done.'

The Professor laid a hand on her arm. 'Please sit down, my dear. The lawyer will keep for another day or so. You need to rest, get your strength back, be strong for the fight.'

'The Professor is right,' Kathryn said, her expression softening. 'If you keel over, you'll be no use to nobody! Me and the others have got a few months yet. Time enough to get it sorted.'

Miranda gave a weak smile and subsided back on to her chair. 'All right then. To return to the previous matter, Teddy might not know about the painting, but he's clearly hedging his bets. If he couldn't find the treasure in the Hall or the grounds, he probably planned to start searching the village properties one by one in the autumn and then sell them for a huge profit.'

'Seems to me we're more than a couple of steps ahead of that nasty piece of work,' Kathryn said. 'No offence,' she added to Miranda.

Miranda waved her words aside. 'None taken. I agree with you. Sadly, my nephew has always been a wastrel. He had every advantage a young man could want and he squandered them all. He has a weakness for playing poker. Unfortunately for him, he's not very good at it. From what I can gather, he owes some rather unpleasant people a lot of money. He's already run through the money his father left him.'

'And now he's got his eyes on Catesby Hall,' Luke said.

Miranda nodded. 'Thank goodness my family never had any truck with primogeniture, otherwise as the surviving male heir he might have had the right to kick me out. As it is, my ownership of Catesby Hall is unassailable, which is why he resorted to other methods to pry it away from me.'

'Well, I need to get back to Harbour Watch,' Kathryn said. She placed her hands on the shoulders of Miranda and the Professor. 'I suggest you two go and relax in the lounge and catch up. I'll be up to fix you some lunch at one.'

Luke stood. 'In the meantime, I'll start searching the attic at Harbour Watch. If I get no joy there, I'll move on to Bill Warren's place. Would you like to join me, Madison?' He angled an eyebrow at her.

'What a splendid idea,' Miranda exclaimed. 'While I'm sure Luke will do a thorough job, I always think it's best to ask a woman to find something.'

Madison painted a smile on her face. 'Happy to help,' she said. A hot, dark attic full of critters and Luke Ryder! What could be more appealing?

8

'Listen, if you're not keen, I'll understand and I won't rat you out to Miranda and the Prof,' Luke said as they walked down the lane ten minutes later.

Although she would have liked nothing better than to spend the day exploring the village, Madison knew the only reason she was here was to help Miranda — and looking for the painting *was* helping her; the fact that she was saddled with a cocky sidekick was just bad luck.

'I want to do this for Miranda,' she replied. She glanced at Luke. Now that they were outside, she could see the livid bruise on his face even more clearly. 'How's your cheek?'

He gave her a rueful smile. 'Sore.'

She nodded. Of course it was. Stupid question. 'I'm sorry Muscles hit you.'

'Muscles?' he repeated, amused.

'It's what I call him.'

Luke laughed. 'I've called him a few things. None as polite as Muscles.'

Madison smiled. She looked at the boats bobbing in the harbour. 'I know you went at Teddy Catesby to draw them away from me. If you hadn't done that, I probably would've been discovered. Thank you.'

'I'm happy to take a punch to the face for you anytime, Madison.'

She waited for the comeback, the rejoinder that would remind her that she now owed him big-time, but none came. Maybe they had got off on the wrong foot. She resolved to make the effort to start over. Stuck in a hot attic with him all day, she probably had little choice anyway.

When they arrived, Luke positioned the stepladder under the attic hatch. Opening the hatch, he flipped a switch and turned the lights on. Madison could see a dull glow from where she stood on the landing. She heard Luke whistle. 'Okay?' she asked.

He bobbed his head down to look at

her. 'We're going to need some sort of lighting rig up here,' he said. 'We'll be okay until mid-afternoon, but after that we won't be able to see a thing.'

Madison thought of the complete and suffocating darkness in the smugglers' tunnel and shivered.

'I'll go and have a word with Charlie up at the garage at lunch time, see if he can spare us any of the lights he uses when he's working under the cars in the inspection pit.' Luke heaved himself into the attic and then looked down at her with a smile. 'One good thing about the gloom — you can't see the spiders.'

Madison pulled a face and Luke laughed. 'Don't worry, Maddy. I'll protect you. I'm your knight in shining armour, remember?'

'Aren't I lucky.' Madison scampered up the stepladder. She had always been a bit of a tomboy; getting dirty didn't bother her, but she could do without little critters scuttling about.

There was a gap between the top of the stepladder and the edge of the boarded-out attic space. Luke reached out a hand. Madison was tempted to ignore the offer and prove she could lever herself in unaided, as he had done, but it seemed petty so she took his hand.

His warm fingers clasped hers and she could see the strong muscles in his forearm working as he helped her up. He didn't strike her as a gym bunny, but he was certainly more powerful than he looked. He swung her up and she teetered forwards into his arms. Reaching out to regain her balance, her hand fell against his chest.

'Steady on, Maddy.' He let go of her hand as his other arm looped around the small of her back, holding her securely. His free hand came up and covered hers where it lay against his chest. 'I'm still a bit sore from where you kicked me there last night.'

'I didn't...' She stopped. *Don't rise to it.*

'Maybe if you were to kiss it better,' he suggested with a grin.

She extracted her fingers from beneath

his, ignoring the fluttering in her stomach at the touch of his hand. 'I've got my balance,' she said. 'You can let go now.'

'You really are very beautiful, Miss Morley.'

Taken by surprise, Madison didn't know how to respond. It was another joke, right? 'And you're a jerk!'

'Very probably.'

He stood her away from him and then as quickly released his grip upon her. He turned to inspect the attic, but not before she saw beneath the cocky look the flash of hurt on his face. Madison was amazed. Damn it all if he hadn't meant it!

It would take her some time to process this new information and determine how best to react to it. She didn't want to hurt Luke's feelings. He was a pain, but his heart was in the right place. She smiled to herself. She knew that for sure; she'd just felt it jumping right out of his chest.

She turned to take in her surroundings. The attic at Harbour Watch had two tiny windows at the front and two at the back. They were grimy with dirt and festooned with cobwebs. Having managed to climb across to one, Luke struggled to open it and finally gave up.

Bare electric bulbs hung in a string down the spine of the attic space, but the torches Luke had grabbed from the under sink cupboard would be invaluable, as even in the daylight many of the recesses of the attic were cloaked in darkness. The scale of the task dawned on Madison and Luke at the same time and they exchanged sympathetic glances.

'Does all this stuff belong to Miranda's family?' Madison asked.

'Not all of it. Ma keeps some bits up here too. Mostly in that back left-hand corner. But the majority belongs to Miranda.'

'We're going to need a plan,' Madison said, hands on hips. She sounded way more confident than she felt.

Luke nodded, stroking his chin. 'I think we should start in the bottom left-hand section and work our way up to the first window on that side. Lucky for us the whole attic has been boarded out,' he said sarcastically, adding, 'It's going to be a long job.'

You can say that again, Madison thought. 'How many properties do the Catesby family own in the village?' she asked hesitantly.

'Best not to dwell on that right now,' Luke said as he started to move boxes out of the way to make a channel to the wall.

'And yet I still want to know. How many?' she persisted.

'Twenty.'

'And this painting, if it does exist, could be in any one of them?' she said, her confidence leaching away to be replaced by dismay.

'That's about the size of it. There is some good news, though.'

'Really?'

'This is by far the biggest of all the properties. We get this one done, we've broken the back of them.' Luke grinned at her.

Swept up by his absurd optimism, Madison mirrored his smile. 'That's all right then,' she replied.

They worked methodically, box by box, inch by inch, to the outside wall, and then back to the middle again. It was hot work, and they were both grateful when Kathryn had the foresight to bring up bottles of water. The attic was full of old furniture, journals and ledgers, paintings and bric-a-brac. For all their diligence, however, they had only covered a small area when they stopped to have a drink.

'Do you think this painting could possibly still exist?' Madison asked. She was sitting opposite him, cross-legged on the wooden boarding. Her jeans were scuffed and dirty, her New York Mets T-shirt a tight distraction. He tried to keep his gaze on her face.

'Realistically? No. But once you hear the story, what person could resist looking?'

She nodded. Her auburn hair was twisted back into a ponytail. He'd been watching it bounce tantalisingly against the nape of her long, slender neck as she'd moved around earlier. How he longed to reach out and stroke that neck, and trace his fingers along the curve of her shoulder. He frowned and looked away. *Too long on your own, son. You really need to get out more.*

'Why did you want to pile up all the paintings we find?' Madison asked.

Luke turned to look at the three paintings they had collected so far. 'I'd like to check them downstairs in proper light, make sure we're not missing something.'

'Like an Old Master?' Madison teased.

'Yeah, wouldn't that be something! No, I'm afraid the idea behind it is a little more prosaic.'

She cocked an eyebrow, waiting for him to continue. Wow, she looked cute when she did that. He forced himself to concentrate. 'Canvases have always been valuable things. Could be someone, years ago, decided to reuse Javier's canvas. It's worth checking.'

'Paint over the original painting, you mean?' Madison asked, dismayed.

'Sometimes. More often they'd turn the canvas and use the other side.'

'So our painting could be hidden inside the frame?'

Our painting. He liked the sound of that. *Our painting* made them sound like a team. He nodded. 'It happens.'

Did she have any idea of the effect she had on him? Of course she did. He'd told her she was beautiful, hadn't he? The words had slipped out before he could stop them. From mind to mouth, bypassing common sense. Her slender body in his arms had felt so good; the perfect O of her mouth as she'd lost her footing; the hitch in her breath as he'd caught her; her warm hand against his chest. It had reminded him of the look of utter relief that had flooded her face when she'd caught sight of him in the smugglers' tunnel the previous evening. His gut twisted even now at the memory.

It had taken every last bit of his restraint not to press his mouth down on hers and kiss her, last night and this morning. At least he had held back. Thank goodness for small mercies, he mused. He'd done enough damage already, making an idiot of himself by betraying his true feelings. It never ended well when he did that. Besides, she'd made her own feelings plain. It was a dead end. No point going there. She'd called him a jerk. She was right. He was. He'd just have to settle for capturing Madison Morley in the pages of his sketchbook. He consoled himself with the thought that it would be fun to choose the best sketch and work it up on canvas after she'd left.

'Why are you staring at me like that?' Madison asked, a hint of alarm in her voice.

Luke was taken aback. 'Was I? Sorry. Just thinking.' He moved his gaze pointedly to the dusty floor.

'Have you always lived in Penrowan?' she asked.

'Pretty much.'

'Have you never wanted to leave?'

'Now and then.' He heard her laugh and looked up.

'Not exactly loquacious, are you?'

Luke smiled. 'How do you know I know what 'loquacious' means?'

'Do you?'

'I might.'

Madison smiled. 'I'll take that as a yes. I had a look at the books in your bookcase. You've got quite a collection.'

'Doesn't mean I've read them. Maybe I bought them as a job lot, make the place look good,' he shot back with a grin.

'They were arranged by subject matter or genre, and then by author, and then by size. If they were just an interior design statement, I'd say you took a lot of trouble over them.'

He smiled. She was good. 'What else did you notice?' He was unashamedly fishing for compliments now. In his experience, that never normally ended well either.

'Good eye for colour. Interesting artwork on the walls, but that's not surprising given that there were a large number of books on art and artists in the bookcase under the stairs. Impressionists, mainly.'

Wow. She really had been taking notice. Just as well she hadn't looked in his fridge the day before the Professor's arrival. She'd have found six bottles of beer and three ready meals. Not to mention the takeaway wrappers in the bin. Cooking always seemed too much trouble when you lived on your own.

'What do you do in New York?' He glanced down at her T-shirt and tried not to notice the rise of her chest. 'Private detective?'

She laughed. 'I used to be a conservator at the New York Museum of Modern Art.'

No wonder she'd picked up on his art books. 'I'm impressed.'

'Don't be. They fired me.'

'I'm sorry.'

She shrugged. 'Couldn't really afford to live in New York anymore, anyway. Not after ...'

'Not after what?' he fished.

'It doesn't matter.'

She looked so sad all of a sudden. Luke felt his heart contract. That will be the broken marriage, he thought. The Professor had told his mother about it over supper last night. Some scumbag city slicker had done the dirty on her by sleeping with a junior associate in the investment bank where he worked. A friend of a friend had spotted them all over each other in a hotel lobby and had felt a duty to tell Madison all about it. Luke imagined there had been a certain amount of relish involved. A nasty business. He couldn't imagine how anyone lucky enough to be in a relationship with Madison could even think about treating her that way. Some men didn't know they were born.

'So where do you live now?' he asked.

'For the next couple of months I'll be in London helping Pop. After that? I don't know.'

'World's your oyster.'

She smiled. 'Something like that. How about you? Can you ever see yourself leaving Penrowan?'

'Probably not.' He knew he sounded like a country hick, lacking in ambition — nothing like the driven, high-achieving crowd she was used to, but there was no point dressing it up.

'And what do you do here in Penrowan?'

'This and that.'

'Wow, you're like an open book.'

He smiled.

'You get a pension and benefits with that?' she joked.

'Oh sure. Plus they throw in a damn fine view of the sea from my office window.'

'As offices go, you do have a pretty good outlook on the world,' she admitted with a smile. 'Well, I guess we'd better get back to work.' She stood and dusted herself off, then stopped and shook her head. 'Why am I bothering?'

Luke smiled. He stepped back to let her go first. She turned, her ponytail brushing her skin in a way that made his heart stop. 'This was nice,' she said.

He nodded. 'Yes, it was.'

Maybe, just maybe, she was beginning to think he wasn't such a jerk after all.

9

'Hi, Pop. I thought I'd come and have lunch with you,' Madison said as the Professor opened the door of Rock Cottage.

'I'm afraid you're a little late, my dear. Kathryn has already made Miranda and me a fine lunch of fresh lemon sole, landed at Tregelian this morning, but I'm having a cup of Darjeeling on the terrace. You're welcome to join me.'

He took another mug down from the cupboard and poured Madison's tea. She sat at the table on the terrace and unwrapped the cheese and pickle sandwiches she'd purchased at the baker's. 'Where's Miranda?'

'Having a little sleep. This has really knocked the stuffing out of her. Not that she'd admit that, of course. How goes the hunt?'

'Hot and slow,' Madison said as she

took a bite of her sandwich.

The Professor nodded. 'It's a hunt for the proverbial needle in a haystack, I grant you.'

'Do you think we'll find anything?'

The Professor squinted across the harbour. 'I'd say the odds are stacked against us, Stick, but we have to try. I thought you might be having lunch with Luke. Don't tell me you two have had a falling out?'

'What? No. He's gone to see someone called Charlie about lending us some lights for the attic.'

'That's all right, then. Can't have any discord in the camp. It would be a terrible shame, particularly when you and Luke have been getting on so well.' His eyes twinkled as he looked at Madison.

Miranda! She'd clearly put two and two together from the boat ride the previous evening, and come up with five. Madison could imagine her and her grandfather having a good old gossip this morning.

'Whatever you're about to say, don't say it!' Madison warned.

The Professor held up his hands in surrender.

She finished her sandwich, enjoying the panoramic view of the bustling harbour. The water was so clear that she could see the seaweed on the sandy bottom being washed back and forth by the current. She smiled at her grandfather as she picked up her mug of tea.

'I was just thinking it might be quite nice for you and Luke to spend some time together, that was all. Take your mind off things.'

'There's no need. I'm fine.'

'Now Stick, we both know that's not true. When you love someone like you loved Will, you love with all your heart. You need time to heal. But there's no rule that says you can't have a little fun at the same time. We should all make time for that. Luke could show you the bright lights of Penrowan.'

Madison raised her eyebrows. 'Are there any?'

'Goodness, yes. You should see the Smugglers' Inn on a Friday night.'

She laughed. 'Thank you for caring, but I don't need you and Miranda acting as some kind of matchmaking service. Particularly not when it comes to Luke Ryder. Did you know he'd been married twice already?'

'Oh yes. But you shouldn't let that put you off. Luke was the injured party on both occasions.'

Madison had a hard time processing that. 'Really?' The word dripped with scepticism.

'Really,' the Professor confirmed. 'I never met his first wife, Georgia, but I did meet his second, Melissa. She seemed like a nice girl, but she treated him shabbily. Anyhow, message received, loud and clear. You want us to stay out of it.' He laughed. 'I shall relay the sentiment to Miranda, and we'll let you two young people sort things out amongst yourselves.'

'There's nothing to sort out,' Madison said, exasperated.

The Professor tapped the side of his nose. 'Mum's the word.'

He really was impossible. 'The two of you seem to have spent a long time talking about me and Luke,' she mused.

Her grandfather nodded. 'Sometimes it's easier to talk about others rather than tackle the elephant in the room.' He gave her a rueful smile.

'You said she was the love of your life.'

'Absolutely. No offence to your dear departed grandmother, but Miranda was the first woman I ever really cared for. I left a piece of my heart with her when I left Penrowan.'

'May I ask what happened, or would you rather not say?' Madison asked gently.

'As I've told you, we spent two glorious summers together. At the end of it, Miranda asked me to stay in Penrowan with her. I couldn't do it, Madison. I've always had wanderlust in my soul. There are so many countries to visit, so many cultures to absorb oneself within. I could never be happy staying in one place for too long.'

'Couldn't Miranda have travelled with you?'

'Sadly, no. It was never on the cards. Her father had already determined that his son, Teddy's father, Edward Senior, was a spendthrift. He'd pinned his hopes on Miranda being his sole heir. As such, he was already starting to train her to run the Catesby estate. There's the Hall, all the properties in the village that you already know about, plus hundreds of acres of farmland, much of it rented out to tenant farmers. Running the whole endeavour is a full-time job. Miranda was born to run the Catesby estate, by heritage but also by temperament. Her heart is here in Penrowan. It always was. She could no more entertain the idea of spending ten months of the year living out of a suitcase in far-flung parts of the world than I could staying put.'

'So you ended it?'

Her grandfather nodded. 'We loved each other, but there was no way we could forge a life together without one of us having to compromise so much of what made life precious to us in the first place. If we'd tried, we would've grown resentful and bitter. It would only have been a question of time. Better to make one sharp cut than suffer a hundred smaller ones to reach the same end. I did keep in touch with several friends in the village, and through them I learned of the death of Miranda's father and her marriage to Mitchell Penrose.'

'Did you ever come back?'

'Not for a long while.' Her grandfather stared across the water. 'I couldn't bear the thought that I might bump into them in the village, hand in hand. Even after I met your grandmother, it would have been too painful, so I stayed away. Mitchell died just over ten years ago. I started coming back here then.'

'And yet you never sought out Miranda?'

'Goodness, no. And as luck or fate would have it, our paths never crossed.'

'Until her letters arrived.'

'Exactly. When a friend as dear as that asks for your help, you should never refuse.'

Madison reached across and squeezed his hand. 'I'm glad we came here,' she said.

The Professor nodded. 'Me, too.'

Madison stood. 'I'd better make my way back. Say hello to Miranda for me when she wakes up.'

'Will do.' The Professor stood.

As Madison crossed the lounge heading towards the front door, she paused in front of the painting of a storm-lashed Penrowan harbour that hung above the fireplace.

'Magnificent painting, isn't it?' the Professor commented.

Madison nodded. 'Striking,' she agreed. 'You can almost taste the salt-water spray hitting your face and feel the wind pummelling you. It's very powerful. Is it by a local artist?'

'Very local.' The Professor's eyes sparkled with jollity. 'It's one of Luke's.'

Astonished, Madison turned back to the picture. 'I didn't even know he painted. He's really talented, Pop.'

'Don't have to tell me, Stick. I've got two Luke Ryder originals hanging in my study in London. One is of Wheal Coates Tin Mine, and the other, larger, one is a painting of the fields above Penrowan, looking out to sea.'

Madison nodded. 'I remember them well. I particularly love the one looking out to sea. Luke did those, too?' she said almost to herself. 'Does he exhibit?'

'Yes. He has various paintings in shops and galleries along the coast, but it's not enough to pay the bills, so he can't paint full-time.'

'How sad. Where did he study art, do you know?'

'London. He won a place at St Martins.'

Madison was impressed. 'That was an achievement in itself,' she said.

Her grandfather nodded. 'Which made it all the more sad when circumstances conspired to bring him back here just a year into his three-year course.'

'Circumstances?' Madison queried.

'He hasn't told you about the accident, what happened to his father and his brother?'

'No,' she said, watching her grandfather suck in his lower lip.

'Can't say I'm surprised. I know he finds it hard to talk about, even after all this time.' He patted her hand. 'Best I let Luke tell you about it when he's ready, my dear.'

'Yes, of course.' Frustrated, Madison burned to know more, even though she knew it wouldn't be right to press her grandfather further. She couldn't help wondering if the time would ever be right for Luke to tell her about it himself.

She stared once more at the painting. There was no denying the man who painted this picture had romance in his soul. It just took a bit of adjustment to get used to the idea that that man was Luke Ryder.

* * *

Madison walked down Pennycombe Lane, busy replaying her conversation with Luke from earlier that morning. He had never given any hint about his work as they had spoken, even when she'd commented about his books on art. She struggled to recall how she had described the artwork on his walls. Impressive? No, she hadn't been that fulsome. Interesting — that had been the word she had used. Maybe that was why he had held back. 'Interesting' could have many connotations. He hadn't pushed her on it. If it had been the other way round, she would have asked, 'Interesting how?' or 'Interesting bad or interesting good?' He had just taken her comment and moved on. She would have to find a way to bring the subject up again.

'Miss Morley? Madison Morley?'

She turned to find Muscles just a couple of feet behind her. She swallowed. *He doesn't know you, remember? He never saw you last night.* She forced what she hoped was a quizzical look onto her face. 'Yes?'

'Granddaughter of Compton Morley?'

She nodded warily. 'Yes.'

'My employer would like a brief word with you, if that's all right? He's waiting for us in a cottage in Lower Dale.'

'I'm sorry, do I know you?' Madison

asked, her voice rising a notch.

'No, but my employer is Mr Catesby of Catesby Hall here in Penrowan.'

'Catesby?' Madison hoped she hadn't overdone the confused look. 'I'm sorry, I don't know a Mr Catesby.'

'His elderly aunt has gone missing and he's very worried about her.'

'I'm sorry to hear that, but I don't see how I can help.'

'Compton Morley is one of Mr Catesby's aunt's oldest friends.'

'Well then, surely it's my grandfather you need to talk to.'

'Indeed, yes. Can you tell me where he is?'

She caught the flash of eagerness that he was a little late in hiding. 'My grandfather got called back to London unexpectedly,' Madison said. Off-season, the streets were worryingly quiet. She edged away.

'When will he be back?'

'Not for a week or so.'

'Would you mind coming and telling Mr Catesby that?'

'No, I'm sorry,' Madison said. 'I have

a friend who's expecting me. In fact, I really must rush.'

Belying his size, Muscles reached out with lightning speed to grab her elbow. 'It'll only take a minute. The cottage is just along here,' he said with a smile, leading her forcibly up a narrow lane.

'I'm sorry, I really cannot come with you. Please let go of my arm.' Madison tried to pull herself free.

'I'm afraid I can't do that, Miss Morley.' Muscles flashed the flick knife that was concealed in his other hand. 'We don't want a scene, do we? My employer just wants a friendly little chat. It won't take long.'

Madison found herself being pulled along the narrow lane, which had squat cottages on either side. There was no one to hear her call out, and Muscles made sure Madison could see the flash of his knife in the sunlight. They stopped in front of a whitewashed stone cottage with a green front door which opened as they approached.

'Miss Morley, I presume?'

'And you must be Mr Catesby,' Madison replied, instantly recognising him but hoping nothing in her voice or her demeanour betrayed that fact. 'Please tell your employee to get his hands off me.'

Catesby waved his hand in a desultory fashion and Muscles immediately released Madison's arm, but moved to stand directly behind her, ready to spring into action if she bolted.

Catesby took a step back and ushered Madison into the cottage.

'My mother always told me not to be alone with strange men,' she said as boldly as she could. 'Whatever you have to say to me, you can do so right here.'

Catesby tutted and Madison felt a nudge in the small of her back from Muscles. She held her ground and the nudge became a shove, driving her forwards.

'There is no need for things to become unpleasant, Miss Morley.'

'I've got news for you, pal. Things became unpleasant the minute your gorilla here pulled a knife on me.'

'I'm sure it was an unfortunate necessity. He can sometimes be a little over-zealous. Now, please...' Catesby moved into the dark interior of the cottage.

Madison half-turned, to be met with Muscles' broad shoulders behind her. There was no escape. She stepped across the threshold and followed Catesby down the hall and into the front room. Muscles stood guard in the doorway.

'I'm sorry to hear about the disappearance of your aunt,' Madison began, 'but as I was telling your man here, my grandfather was called away unexpectedly on urgent business. He'll be gone for about a week.' She saw the muscles in Catesby's jaw clench.

'Where?'

'I'm sorry?'

'Where has your grandfather gone?'

'I don't see that that's any of your business, Mr Catesby,' Madison said imperiously.

'She told me London,' Muscles said.

'So he's gone home?'

Madison had visions of this man and

his friends turning up at her grandfather's elegant west London home and ransacking the place. 'Briefly, to pick up some papers, and then on to Oxford,' Madison said, improvising. 'I can pass on a message,' she offered. 'But as he's never mentioned anyone called Catesby to me, I'm not sure how he can help you.'

'Why did he leave you behind?'

'We'd only just arrived. He said I needed a holiday and that I should stay and he'd be back soon. Look, if your aunt has gone missing, surely you should be talking to the police, not me?'

Catesby narrowed his eyes. 'My aunt is very precious to me, but sadly she's elderly and very confused. She has dementia and is given to bouts of paranoia. I don't think the police would be very interested in helping me when no crime has been committed.'

Catesby's gaze was sharp, sweeping her features for the slightest sign that she knew a terrible wrong had been committed here. Madison prayed her expression stayed neutral.

'I'm very worried about her. Please, Miss Morley, if you've seen my aunt, could you tell me where she is?' Catesby placed his hand on Madison's arm, but his touch was dry and light, there was no malice in it. 'I really am very worried about her. I know Compton Morley is one of her oldest friends, and when I heard he was in the village, I felt sure my aunt would have sought him out. Did she? Have they left together?'

Madison stared into Catesby's light blue eyes. 'I saw my grandfather off, and when he left, he was alone. As far as I'm aware, I've never even met your aunt, but the next time I speak to my grandfather I'll ask him.'

Catesby nodded and released his grip. 'I'd be most grateful.'

Madison turned to leave.

'You're staying at Harbour Watch, aren't you?'

'Yes, that's right.'

'No doubt you've met Kathryn's son, Luke?'

'Yes, he brought my grandfather and

me down to the village from the station.'

Catesby gave a cold smile. 'Luke and I go back a long way. In fact, I had to throw him off my property last night for trespass and assault. I'd be very careful not to associate too closely with Luke Ryder if I were you, Miss Morley. The man is trouble.'

'I'll bear that in mind,' Madison said curtly. She stared at Muscles, who looked at Catesby over her shoulder. He obviously gave the man a sign, because Muscles moved aside to let Madison pass.

She fought the urge to break into a run as she walked back along the hallway to the open front door. The street beyond was an oasis of calm in the bright sunshine and she was eager to escape the depths of the gloomy cottage.

'Miss Morley?'

Madison was tempted to keep on walking and ignore him, but curiosity got the better of her and she turned. 'Yes?'

'Please forgive my heavy-handedness. I really am beside myself with worry over my aunt's whereabouts.'

I bet you are, Madison thought, *not out of love, but because you're afraid she holds the key to a fortune that might slip through your fingers. What a snake!*

'You'll contact me if you hear anything, or if your grandfather knows anything?' Catesby persisted. He took a card from his pocket and passed it to her.

The card read 'Teddy Catesby, Catesby Hall'. Madison felt her anger spike on Miranda's behalf. This interloper had not only moved into Miranda's home and made her a prisoner inside it, but he was clearly now setting himself up as the new owner. It was all she could do not to screw the card up and throw it back at him, but she knew she must keep up appearances. 'If I hear anything, I'll let you know.' She put the card in the pocket of her jeans.

'Bless you, Miss Morley. I hope we meet again in better circumstances.' He gave her an oily smile. 'Perhaps my wife and I can entertain you at Catesby Hall? Perhaps supper one evening?'

Frankly, I'd rather stick pins in my

eyes, Madison thought.

'The Hall is an interesting building,' Catesby continued. His smile became almost genuine. 'I do hope you'll feel able to visit us during your stay.'

'I really must be going,' Madison said forcefully.

'Of course. I've detained you long enough.'

Madison strode out into the sunshine and made her way back to Fore Street. She had the feeling that Teddy Catesby's gaze followed her until she was out of sight.

Once on Fore Street, Madison refrained from launching into a run. She was in two minds. Should she head to Harbour Watch and tell Luke what had happened, or go back to Rock Cottage and tell her grandfather? She decided that Catesby or Muscles might be following her and that it would look suspicious if she went back to Rock Cottage. Better to let Luke go home to warn her grandfather and Miranda to keep out of sight.

Fortunately, Luke was sitting in the kitchen with his mother when she arrived.

Kathryn pushed a plate of biscuits towards Madison as she sat down. 'Lemon shortbread, made them this morning. Please help yourself, my lovely.'

'Thank you,' Madison said, astonished to see her hand was shaking as she reached for a biscuit.

'Are you okay?' Luke asked, instantly picking up on her discomfort.

Safe now inside the homely kitchen, Madison felt tears prick her eyes. She didn't want to cry in front of Luke, she really didn't. She nodded, and only once she was sure she had got her emotions under control did she begin to recount what had happened.

Kathryn draped a sympathetic arm over her shoulders as she spoke. 'You must have been terrified, my lovely.'

Luke's face darkened with anger. 'He's gone too far this time. Ordering his thug to lamp me is one thing, but threatening Madison — '

'He didn't threaten me exactly,' Madison said quickly.

'The guy pulled a knife on you.'

'Catesby said he'd been overzealous.'

Luke snorted. 'Man needs teaching a lesson. He was waiting in a cottage in Lower Dale, you say?'

Madison nodded.

Luke looked at Kathryn. 'That'll be John Parsons' place. John died a couple of months ago,' he added for Madison's benefit. 'Looks like Catesby's already taken possession. Guess that's one attic we can cross off our list.' He went to stand up. 'I'm going to have it out with him.'

Madison shot out her hand to cover Luke's. 'No! Wait!' She saw his gaze fall to her hand over his. Embarrassed, she withdrew it. 'He doesn't know if I was telling the truth or not. Better that you go up to Rock Cottage and tell Pop and Miranda to keep out of sight. It'll buy us a few more days to carry on searching. If you antagonise him, it could make life more difficult for us.'

'If *I* antagonise *him*?' Luke repeated indignantly.

'I'd like nothing better than to give

him a piece of my mind,' Madison said. 'But it's not a good idea, not in the circumstances.'

'She's right,' Kathryn said softly as she relinquished her hold on Madison, and placed a hand on Luke's shoulder instead, before she went back to the washing up.

'Yeah, I know she's right,' Luke conceded.

'He'll get what's coming to him,' Madison continued. 'We'll see to that.'

Luke pushed a hand through his hair and then nodded. 'Okay. I'll nip home and tell the Prof and Miranda to keep a low profile. You stay here,' he said, pointing to Madison.

She nodded. She had no intention of wandering around Penrowan in the immediate future. The encounter with Muscles and Catesby had shaken her more than she cared to admit. If things had turned nasty, she would not have been able to escape from that cottage. This time she had been lucky. She prayed there wouldn't be a next time.

Luke put his hand on her shoulder

as he passed by. 'Sure you're okay?' he asked.

Feeling much stronger now, she nodded. 'I'm fine,' she assured him. 'Honestly.'

He gave her a tight smile, squeezed her shoulder, and then gave it a couple of quick pats before heading out of the door.

★   ★   ★

The lights Luke had managed to procure from Charlie had done the trick. He had threaded them across the roof rafters so that they hung down over the area of the attic they were working in, and for the first time Madison could see right to the edge of the attic and the shadows that licked up the walls.

They had resumed their search on Luke's return from Rock Cottage. By all accounts, it had taken some time to calm her grandfather and Miranda down, so outraged were they by the attack on Madison. With the perspective of time, she was now beginning to wonder if she had let her imagination carry her away. If she had stood her ground with Muscles, would he really, in broad daylight, have carried her off or cut her? She doubted it.

'Penny for them?' Luke asked.

Madison told him what was on her mind.

'Don't doubt yourself,' Luke said quickly. 'You were threatened. He grabbed you by the elbow and dragged you along the street. That's assault, however you dress it up.'

Madison nodded. 'Thanks,' she said quietly. 'I keep going over it in my mind. Should I have done this? Should I have said that?'

Luke rocked back on his haunches, putting down the books he had been flicking through. 'You did brilliantly, and with a bit of luck your nifty bit of misinformation will keep Catesby off our backs for a few days.'

'He really doesn't like you, you know,' Madison said.

Luke laughed. 'Good. The feeling's mutual.' He picked up another box and began rooting round in it. 'What did he say about me?' he asked a few minutes later.

'He said you were trouble and I shouldn't associate too closely with you.'

Luke chortled. His rich, warm laugh seemed to rise up and fill the attic space. 'Are you inclined to believe him?'

Madison smiled. 'As you haven't pulled a knife on me or ordered anyone else to do so, I'd say you were in the clear. So far,' she added with a grin.

10

Luke hit the backlight on his watch. It was six forty. He stood and dusted off his jeans. 'Time to pack up, I think, Madison.'

She nodded, head down over a packing case.

'It'll still be there tomorrow,' he said.

She looked up and smiled. 'More's the pity.' She stretched her arms above her head and eased out the kinks in her back.

Luke studiously averted his gaze, concentrating instead on the handful of paintings they had discovered. He was keen to get them downstairs and examine them more closely. 'If you've had enough, I can carry on tomorrow,' he offered, glancing back.

She was standing now, hands on hips, surveying the attic. 'Not a chance, buster! I wouldn't want to risk missing the magic moment.'

They looked at each other and laughed.

'Supper will be ready at seven,' Kathryn said, suddenly popping her head through the open hatchway. 'Just enough time for the two of you to come down and freshen up. The Tregelian Suite is free, Luke, if you want a shower.'

'Thanks, Mum.'

He watched Madison descend the ladder and then handed her down the five canvases they had collected. As he jumped down onto the landing, he quickly flicked through the paintings once more. There was nothing immediately suspicious about them, and they did not look particularly old, but first appearances could be deceptive. He propped them up against the banister. 'See you in twenty minutes,' he said to Madison.

She nodded and disappeared into her room. Luke trotted along to the Tregelian Suite. Thank goodness it was still so early in the season and his mother wasn't inundated with visitors. He always kept a wash bag of essentials at her place, and a change of clothes in case the weather changed while he was out on one of the boats and got a drenching. He was pleased to see his mother had put his things on the bed along with a fresh towel.

Dusty and hot from toiling in the attic, the shower felt cool and invigorating. The tiredness that had seemed so enervating was now sloughing off him along with the soap suds, and he felt re-energised when he emerged from the shower cubicle. Slinging the towel around his waist, he looked at his reflection in the bathroom mirror. Catesby's thug had done a proper job on his face. The lump had risen and was thicker than the last time he'd looked at it, and the bruising was coming out more fully now too, spreading under his eye and in the opposite direction into his hairline. It was a livid purple, splintering into black in places.

Despite the battering he had taken, Luke had meant what he said about being prepared to have it out with Catesby and his thug. When he thought about what they had done to Madison, his blood boiled. The man was ready to walk over anyone who might get in his way. Luke knew he should be under no illusions as to what Catesby was capable of. If he could hold his own aunt prisoner and drug her like that, there was no telling how far he would go, but even so Luke had not considered any of them might be in danger once they got Miranda back to the village. He had clearly been naïve.

He remembered the way Madison's hand had shaken as she had recounted what had happened to her. That lady was one tough cookie, but she had been scared. He could tell she had been fighting back the tears. It was the shock probably, coming out after the attack. He had longed to gather her up and hold her in his arms; to tell her she was safe and that he, Luke Ryder, would not let any harm come to her. Instead, all he had done was pat her shoulder. Pathetic!

He shook his head and, rubbing his chin, gave himself a rueful look. He hadn't fallen this hard or this fast for anyone since Melissa. And look how well that turned out! Better to consign Madison to the what-might-have-beens. He wasn't interested in a fling; there had been enough of those. What he wanted was someone to share his life with. Madison, with her high-flying career, albeit temporarily on hold, and her sassy big-city ways, would not be a stayer. Penrowan would be too small to contain a woman of such spirit. And that was assuming she'd be interested in him in the first place.

'Big assumption,' he said aloud.

'Who are you talking to?' Kathryn asked from the bedroom.

'Myself,' Luke replied. 'You shouldn't go sneaking up on people like that, Ma.'

'I wasn't sneaking,' Kathryn said indignantly. 'I was coming to tell you there's a chicken in the oven that needs carving when you're dressed, and there's a nice bottle of white and a strawberry cheesecake in the fridge.'

Luke smiled. 'Are we setting out to impress anyone in particular?' he teased.

'I'm not. You are. I'm having dinner with the Professor and Miranda. You, meanwhile, are going to entertain our young guest with your sparkling and witty conversation over dinner.'

Luke pulled a face. 'Why do I feel like I'm being set up?'

'Nonsense,' Kathryn replied. 'I'm just giving you two young people a chance to get to know each other.' She reached out to stroke her son's chin. 'You really are very handsome, you know.'

'For goodness sake, Ma!' Luke ducked away.

'What? You may be taller than me, my darling, but you'll always be my little boy. I just want you to be happy,' she added.

'I am happy,' he replied.

Kathryn shook her head vigorously. 'I want to see you properly happy,' she said. 'Settled with a nice girl and a couple of children, happy.'

'How do you know that'll make me happy?'

'Because you're not right now. You mustn't let what happened with Melissa and Georgia put you off. They were never good enough for you.'

Luke laughed. 'No one would ever be good enough in your eyes, Ma.'

She nodded and, catching his hand, squeezed it between hers. 'You gave up so much to come home when I needed you, darling.' She brought his hand up to her lips and kissed it. 'I'll never forget what you did for me.'

'I'd do the same tomorrow, Ma.'

She stroked his face. 'Yes, I believe you would. Your dad would be very proud. Well, I'd better get off. Enjoy yourselves.'

'Ma, wait! I'm not happy about you walking up Pennycombe on your own. Look what happened to Madison earlier. Let me get dressed and I'll walk with you.'

'What about the chicken?'

'I'm sure the chicken can look after itself,' he replied sardonically.

'Funny,' Kathryn said. 'There's no need,' she protested.

'Let me do it for my own peace of mind, then,' Luke countered.

Reluctantly, Kathryn nodded.

'I'll let Madison know what I'm doing and be back to carve the chicken in no time,' he said with a wink.

While his mother waited for him downstairs, Luke knocked on Madison's bedroom door.

'Just a minute,' she called.

She pulled the door back a moment later. She was dressed in one of the fluffy white bathrobes his mother supplied, cinched in tightly at the waist, her wet hair hanging around her shoulders. Luke could see the slight curve of her collarbone in the V of the dressing gown and longed to move his lips along its fragile length, kissing the hollow in the centre of her throat and then making his way up to her mouth. He swallowed.

'Did you want something?' Madison asked.

'Yes. Sorry. I just wanted to let you know Mum's going up to Rock Cottage to have supper with the Professor and Miranda. I don't want her walking up there on her own, not after what happened to you, so I'm going to walk with her.' He could see the shadow fall across her eyes as he spoke. It would take a long time for her to get over being grabbed like that.

'That's a good idea,' she said. 'Circle the wagons.'

'I'm sorry?'

'Like the cowboys used to do in the old days. Circle the wagons to protect the people inside the circle from attack.'

'Right. I'll be back soon.'

'Don't rush on my account.'

Not exactly falling over herself to have dinner with you, is she? Luke stuck his head into the kitchen. His mother had lit candles. Candles! And the best silver cutlery was out. He rubbed his eyes, suddenly feeling tired again.

'Don't you change a thing!' Kathryn said sternly from the doorway.

'Candles? Seriously?'

'It's all about ambience,' she said as they headed down the stairs to the front door.

'I'll give you ambience,' Luke tutted.

Candles? Madison surveyed the kitchen in astonishment. Her grandfather and Miranda had clearly decided to let Kathryn in on their wild theories about her and Luke. So much for letting them get on with it themselves, as her grandfather had promised. Not that there was anything to get on with, Madison thought as she took the chicken out of the oven and set about carving it.

Rain lashed the kitchen window and she smiled, thinking of Kathryn's warning about a mackerel sky that morning. She heard the front door go a few minutes later and the sound of someone running up the stairs from the basement. A frisson of fear ran through her. What if it wasn't Luke? What if Catesby or Muscles had decided to be unbelievably bold? She took up the knife she had used to carve the chicken.

Luke opened the door and relief flooded onto Madison's face. She put down the knife.

'You okay?'

'For a moment I wondered if Catesby or Muscles had got into the house,' she admitted.

'Oh Madison...' Luke raked a hand through his wet hair. 'They wouldn't break in here — they wouldn't dare.' He strode across the kitchen to stand beside her.

For a moment she thought he was going to hug her, but then he gently placed his hand on her forearm. It was the lightest of touches and then it was gone, but it was enough to set her nerve endings fizzing.

'You're safe here.'

Madison nodded. She suspected it would take her a long time to feel safe anywhere.

'I see you started dishing up.'

'Your mother's done us a magnificent feast. There's wine in the fridge.'

'I know, she told me.' Luke pulled a face. 'I'm sorry about all this.' He waved his hand over the table.

Madison laughed. 'My grandfather, your mother and Miranda seem to have got the wrong idea about us.'

'Absolutely.' Luke nodded vigorously. 'Embarrassing, isn't it?'

'A bit.'

'We don't have to indulge their fantasies about some romantic entanglement, but that doesn't mean we can't enjoy a nice meal together,' he added reasonably.

'My thoughts exactly,' Madison agreed.

'Shall we lose the candles, but keep the wine?'

'I like your thinking.'

Madison watched Luke uncork the wine and pour them both a glass as she put their plates on the table. He was dressed in cream chinos and a white short-sleeved shirt. It was the smartest she had ever seen him. She looked down at her own three-quarter-length sage-green trousers and plain white T-shirt. She had resisted the urge to dress up so as not to encourage him, but now she felt underdressed and a little foolish.

The scent of the extinguished candles was pleasant. Madison felt more comfortable with them snuffed out. Life was complicated enough right now without the prospect of getting involved with someone. Thank goodness Luke was on the same page as her.

Or was he? While he was clearly embarrassed at being set up, she remembered the way his gaze had devoured her bare skin when she'd opened her bedroom door. He'd practically been struck dumb by the sight of her. And her own heart had thumped with excitement as he'd looked at her with such unabashed admiration. She'd almost forgotten what it felt like to be the centre of someone's attention like that. For a heartbeat, she had wondered if Luke would step across the threshold and kiss her, and in the next heartbeat she'd wondered whether she would let him.

Tread lightly, Madison, she warned herself. In her vulnerable state it would be all too easy to fall for someone like Luke Ryder with his easygoing smile, his strength and stability. She felt the flutter of attraction once more in her stomach, the butterfly's wings of anticipation against her ribcage. It would be nice to have a warm hand in hers as she strolled along the pavement; someone to share stories with. She missed having a confidante: a cuddle on the sofa in front of the television, a reassuring kiss on the cheek, an encouraging smile. The simplest of things that she had taken for granted when married to Will. How quickly it could all slip away. *And let's not even get started on the sex.* She missed the intimacy as much as the hot kisses and hungry hands, the passion and the excitement. Would she ever be able to trust anyone enough again to let them get that close?

'You're miles away,' Luke observed. 'What were you thinking about?'

Madison choked a little over her wine. If you only knew, she thought. 'Just thinking what a wonderful spread Kathryn has put on for us,' she said, improvising.

She turned her attention to the food. She may have been improvising, but it was still true. Kathryn had cooked them a succulent herby chicken with lemon-flavoured stuffing and roast potatoes that were crunchy on the outside and fluffy inside, together with purple-sprouting broccoli and juicy baby carrots, all topped with a rich chicken gravy.

'I think I've died and gone to food heaven,' Madison said truthfully.

Luke smiled. 'My mother is one hell of a cook.' He lifted his wine glass. 'I propose a toast. To the Spanish galleon.'

Madison picked up her wine glass and tilted it against his. 'To the Spanish galleon, wherever she may be.'

They ate for a few minutes in contented silence, enjoying the food. Madison chased her fringe from her eyes. There were so many questions she wanted to ask Luke, but where to begin?

'I didn't know you were an artist,' she said as an opening gambit.

Luke looked up. 'I'm a man of many talents.' He gave her a self-deprecating smile. 'That just happens to be one of them.'

Madison shook her head. 'I think you're being too modest, Luke. That painting of Penrowan Harbour, the one hanging over your fireplace — there's real talent in every brushstroke.'

'It's very kind of you to say so.' He hung his head, all of his attention directed at his plate. 'Particularly coming from someone like you, with your background,' he mumbled.

Madison was taken aback. Here was a man — no, an *artist* — of incredible talent, who clearly wasn't used to receiving praise for his work.

'There's such power in that painting,' Madison continued, now talking to Luke's bowed head. 'I could almost taste the saltwater on my lips and feel the gale blowing through my hair.' She thought she caught the hint of a smile on his face.

'That's good.' He nodded as if reassuring himself.

She had seen this reaction time and time again in the art world. The ones with real talent doubted themselves, crippled by a lack of confidence, while the confident ones got by with a modicum of talent and a big mouth.

'I was so taken with it,' she said, 'that I asked my grandfather who'd painted it.'

Luke looked up. 'Bet you had a shock.'

'I was surprised, seeing as how you hadn't mentioned it.'

He shrugged. 'Not the kind of thing you drop into the conversation, is it? By the way, I'm an artist. Want to buy a painting?'

Madison smiled. 'Well as it happens, I do, actually.'

Luke's eyes narrowed as he gazed at her. 'Seriously?'

'Seriously,' she confirmed. 'I'd like to buy the one above your fireplace, but I'm guessing that one's not for sale.'

'You'd be right,' he said. 'But I have others like it.'

'Excellent. Do you exhibit?'

He pulled a face. 'I have some paintings on sale or return in a few of the local galleries and shops, and I have some hanging in the permanent art exhibition at the back of the village hall.'

'How about in London?'

'London?' He looked shocked. 'No, never.'

'You should.' She was adamant. 'The

184

quality of that work? They'd snap them up. I've got a friend — '

'Don't, Madison. Thank you, but I'm not really into all that.'

'Into all what?'

'Networking and schmoozing. It's just not me.'

'How do you pay the bills?'

He looked taken aback by her bluntness. 'I decorate people's houses. And when I haven't got a job on, I work on my paintings.'

Remembering Luke's conversation with Mick, Madison wanted to cry with frustration.

'I'm lucky, Penrowan is a thriving tourist spot. The hotels and guest houses like their exteriors to look good each spring after a battering from the gales, and they all need to refurb their rooms on a regular basis so...' He shrugged.

'Do you have studio space?'

'I converted the attic at Rock Cottage, put in a line of sky lights. Proper job,' he declared.

'With your talent, you should be in

there painting all the time. What you need is an agent to do all the networking and schmoozing for you.'

'You offering?' he asked with a grin.

'I hate to see talent not being maximised.'

'Or monetised?' he ventured.

'What's so wrong about being paid a fair price for hard work? You wouldn't paint someone's house and be embarrassed to accept payment for it, but I bet you're undercharging on your paintings all the time.'

He shrugged again, and she could tell he was becoming uncomfortable with the conversation. *Time to back off, Madison.* She took a sip of her wine. When she looked up she found his gaze on hers.

'What you said about the undercharging? You're right.'

'I take it the paintings in my room upstairs and in the corridors here are all Luke Ryder originals?'

He nodded.

'They're very good.'

'But not as good as the picture of

the storm?' he said, picking up on her hesitation.

'Maybe I'm just more in the mood for a stormy scene than happy holiday ones,' Madison countered, drawing the tines of her fork through the rich gravy.

'I heard about what happened. To your marriage, I mean,' Luke said.

'Oh! I'd hoped my grandfather would rather more discreet.'

'I think my mother winkled it out of him, She wanted to know why a pretty woman like you didn't have a rock on her finger.'

'In my opinion, marriage isn't all it's cracked up to be.'

'Hey, you're talking to an expert.'

'Oh yes, I forgot. You see my marriage and raise me by one,' Madison said.

'For what it's worth, I think the guy's a jerk — and if he did that to you, he clearly didn't deserve you in the first place.'

Madison was touched. She took a sip of her wine, although it was hard to swallow over the lump that had suddenly risen in her throat.

'Did you have any idea?' Luke asked gently.

She shook her head. 'I felt such a fool when his colleague told me.' She slapped her hand against her forehead. 'I mean, really — how could I have not known? How naïve was I? Then when the news sank in, I felt my heart splinter into a thousand pieces, and the rest of my world went right along with it.'

'It wasn't naïveté,' Luke replied. 'The guy promised to love and honour you for the rest of his life. You had every right to believe him and trust him,' he said vehemently.

Was he still talking about her, Madison wondered, or had his words been coloured by his own experiences? What was it her grandfather had said? Luke had been the injured party on both occasions.

'Well, I think this is very unfair,' she said. 'You know about my tale of woe, and yet I know nothing of either of yours.'

Luke smiled and sipped his wine. 'How do you know they're tales of woe?' he countered.

'Well, you're not playing happy families up at Rock Cottage for a start, so that's a bit of a giveaway,' she replied.

'Fair point.' He took another sip of his wine.

Madison waited. And waited. Was he going to blow her out and not reciprocate? Oh, come on! That wasn't fair.

'Tell me about life in the Museum of Modern Art,' he said. 'It's somewhere I've always wanted to visit.'

'You paint seascapes with all the assurance of a J.M. Turner or a Winslow Homer. Your house is full of books about impressionist painters like Monet and Renoir, and yet you hanker after modern art. The man is an enigma,' Madison declared.

Luke grinned. 'Moving target, more like,' he asserted. 'Harder to hit, that way.'

They spent a pleasant hour talking about their favourite paintings and artists, places of inspiration and paint techniques. Two slices of cheesecake came out of the fridge and were duly devoured, and the rest of the wine was drunk.

'Do you paint, Madison?' Luke asked her.

She giggled and shook her head vehemently. She'd had a little too much to drink and her head swam from the sudden movement. 'I'm a frustrated artist,' she explained. 'I wish I could do it. I see a beautiful landscape and I ache to capture it on paper, but all I'm able to produce are stick people and rudimentary scenes.'

'It served Lowry well,' Luke pointed out.

'Lowry had talent. All I have is embarrassment. No, I'm happy on the other side of the fence. It's good to know what you're good at and even more important to know what you're bad at. Like marriage,' she added, twisting the stem of her wine glass between her fingers and feeling suddenly morose.

Without warning, Luke grabbed her hand across the table. 'Come on,' he announced, tugging her arm.

Standing, Madison steadied herself against the table. 'Where are we going?'

'Mum's private lounge. We've been

sitting here talking about art for ages. Let's go take a look at what we brought down from the attic today.'

There were five paintings in all: two landscapes, one seascape and two portraits, one of a country gent with a large hound standing to attention at his side, the other a rotund lady in a voluminous dress displaying an extravagant décolletage, her hair pinned up in curls.

'What are we looking for?' Madison asked.

'Something that doesn't look quite right,' Luke replied.

She shot him a look, and watched as he hefted the portrait of the large lady into the air.

'Fancy frame, probably been reused.' He flipped the painting over and, leaning it against the sofa, knelt to press his hands along the backing.

Getting into the spirit of things, Madison knelt beside him. 'There's a label there with old-fashioned copperplate writing. It's quite faded.' She turned her head and squinted at it. 'Says Leonora Catesby.'

'One of the many ladies of Catesby Hall.' Luke turned it the right way round once more and stood it against the wall.

'No good?' Madison asked, disappointed.

'The Catesbys have always had money. If they commissioned a portrait, the artist would not have been reusing old Catesby canvases to paint on.'

'Unless a Catesby painted it themselves,' Madison said.

'It's possible, I suppose.' He stared at Leonora. 'She may not be my cup of tea, but she is well-painted. I don't think an amateur did this.'

He picked up the seascape. It was mid-sized with a plain wooden frame. 'This is interesting.' He carried it over to the light. 'Incredibly dirty. I'm no conservator, but I bet there's a pretty decent painting lurking beneath a couple of hundred years of crud.'

Madison peered over his arm. 'That looks just like Penrowan Head.' She pointed to a slightly less murky area.

'Damn if it isn't,' Luke said. He turned the painting over.

'Anything?' Madison asked.

'Nothing but a few scratches on the frame.' He peered more closely at it. 'Hang on a minute. They're not scratches. I think they might be words.' His voice crept up a notch. 'Your eyes are younger than mine. See if you can make it out while I go hunt out a magnifying glass. I'm sure Ma's got one in the kitchen somewhere.'

Madison took the frame. The scratches just looked like scratches to her. Although … She screwed up her eyes. Did that first set of marks say 'Roses'?

She looked up as Luke returned carrying a magnifying glass. 'I think it may say 'Roses',' she told him.

'I thought I could see a capital R.' He grinned at her. 'We could be on to something, Maddy!' He took the painting back from her and angled the frame on top of the table before moving a lamp from the sideboard and turning the bulb to face the frame. Then he held the magnifying glass above the line of scratches and they both peered down.

Madison could feel Luke's shoulder nudging hers, his beachcomber-blond hair brushing her cheek. He smelt of soap and fabric conditioner. She found it pleasant and reassuring.

Luke turned to her and grinned, and she grinned back. 'You smell nice,' he said.

Flustered, she said, 'It's one of Sarah Jessica Parker's.'

'Does Sarah know you've got it?'

She was just about to explain who Sarah Jessica Parker was when she caught the twinkle in his eye, the slight pull of a smile on his mouth.

'Don't worry, I know who SJP is. I'm a man of the world. I've watched *Sex and the City*. Suits you,' he added.

'Thanks.'

He turned back to the frame. 'Definitely says 'Roses'. That next letter looks like a capital B. I think it's 'Box'.'

'Yes, it is,' Madison said, gripped by excitement. 'And the word next to it is definitely 'Herbs'.'

'So we have Roses, Box, Herbs.'

'Is that it?' Madison said, disappointed.

'There are no more scratches on this side of the frame. Let's check the rest.' He gradually moved the frame round as they scanned it under the magnifying glass. 'Look, there!' He pointed to a new set of scratches directly opposite the others. 'It says, 'He tends them all.' '

"Roses Box Herbs, he tends them all,' ' Madison repeated. 'A gardener? You get box hedging, right?'

Luke nodded. 'Yes, and the kitchen garden at Catesby Hall is bordered by box hedging. They probably grow herbs there as well.'

'So is the treasure buried under the herb garden?' Madison speculated.

'Or the rose beds?' Luke countered. 'And of course we don't know if the gardens are where they were in the 1500s.'

'How can we find out?'

'Miranda will know. There are books on the history of Catesby Hall, plans and diagrams. Miranda's read them all. She's a real student of her own family history and the house. I bet she'll know just what this means. We put it together with the directions in the journal and Bob's your uncle!'

'But how do we know this will lead us to the treasure? We still haven't found the Spanish galleon,' Madison pointed out.

Luke laid the painting down on the table. 'Only one way to find out.' He disappeared from the room and returned carrying a knife.

'What are you going to do?' Madison asked, alarmed.

'Take the painting out of the frame, or at least take the backing off.'

Madison held the painting steady as Luke worked. He had a skilled hand, gently persuading the frame to yield after so many years. Slowly, the backing began to lift. They both saw it at the same time: the ghostly shadow of a painting, a jumble of lines emerging out of a stained and dirty canvas. As their eyes adjusted and began to follow the curve of a sail or the beam of a mast, they discovered the broad planks and fine detail of a long-lost ship; a castle of the sea.

'The Spanish galleon,' Madison said in awe.

'I didn't think it was possible,' Luke said.

'We did it!' Madison said as awe gave way to delight. 'We actually did it!'

'Oh my God!' Luke exclaimed. 'We've found her. We've only gone and bloody found her.' Whooping with joy, he put the painting down and swept Madison into his arms. Lifting her clean off her feet, he swung her round as she cried out in elation.

Madison put her hands on his shoulders as she was hoisted into the air. Could it really be true? A five-hundred-year-old mystery about to be solved, and she and Luke had found the vital component, the needle in the haystack.

As their initial exuberance subsided, Luke came to a halt and set Madison down gently. Her hands stayed on his shoulders. She didn't need them to steady herself, she just liked the way his skin felt through his shirt. Their eyes locked. Madison was conscious of Luke's arms still around her waist, his body pressed to hers. He didn't attempt to step away. She was glad; she didn't want him to.

He opened his mouth to speak, but before he could say anything, on impulse Madison kissed him. It was a fleeting kiss, lips meeting lips, nothing more. She drew back, shocked by her own forthrightness.

He loosed a hand from around her waist and brought it up to brush her hair back from her face. 'Madison …'

She had never heard her name said with such longing. They looked at each other and the air seemed to burn up between them. Then they kissed each other again. And again. Madison felt Luke's hand move into her hair, bunching it up, pulling her closer. His lips danced against her cheeks, her chin and down to her throat. Madison arched her neck, giving herself up to the glory of his mouth on her skin before she went on her own journey of discovery, softly pressing her lips against his Adam's apple, his strong jaw, the prickle of stubble on his chin, the angry bruise along his cheekbone.

This is how it begins, she thought. *This is how it always begins.* Her senses sizzled under his touch, his molten gaze lighting her up as she took in every detail of his handsome face.

She had come here to help her grandfather's friend and found herself caught up in a treasure hunt. Now, here in Luke Ryder's arms, she knew she had found a new sort of treasure, more precious than silver pieces of eight: she'd found a way to mend a broken heart.

The door opened and Luke and Madison immediately fell apart, but not before Kathryn said, 'Well, aren't you two just a picture? Don't stop on my account,' she added quickly. 'I can make myself scarce.'

Luke gave Madison a bashful grin. 'No need, Ma. What are you even doing here? I said I'd come and get you.'

'And you, my dear boy, seem to have

lost track of time — although I can see why.' Kathryn gave Madison a warm smile. 'It's gone eleven. Miranda went to bed at nine. The Professor gamely stayed up with me, but I could see he was waning.'

'You shouldn't have walked back on your own,' Luke said.

Kathryn tutted. 'Born and bred in this village. Know every inch like the back of my hand. Do you honestly think I'm going to let Teddy Catesby or his hireling stop me doing what I've always done? I've known Teddy since he was knee high to a gnat. He doesn't scare me.'

Madison kept a diplomatic silence. Luke threw her a look followed by a smile. Out of sight of his mother, his fingers closed around hers and gave them a squeeze.

'His hireling frightened Madison, Ma. Don't underestimate him.'

'Okay, okay.' Kathryn held up her hand in surrender. 'Why have you torn the backing off that painting?' she asked in surprise.

Luke and Madison grinned at each other.

'We've found it, Ma. We've found the Spanish galleon and some kind of verse. I'm sure Miranda will know what it means.'

'You've found the galleon?' Kathryn said, her voice lifting in awe as she clapped her hands to her mouth. 'I thought it was all a fairy story,' she conceded. 'I never actually thought you'd find it. Let me see,' she cried.

Luke stood back, allowing his mother to examine the ancient painting while Madison recited the verse.

Kathryn stroked Luke's battered face. 'One way or another, I get the feeling Teddy Catesby's going to be out of all our lives soon.'

Luke smiled. 'All we have to do now is find the treasure!'

11

"Roses Box Herbs. He tends them all,' '
Miranda recited.

It was mid-afternoon, and they were
gathered around Luke's kitchen table as
rain lashed the window. The wind was up,
and the fishing vessels and pleasure boats
were being tossed around on the choppy
harbour waters. Miranda had been ensconced with her lawyer all morning, and
this was the first opportunity Luke and
Madison had had to share their discovery.

'We were thinking maybe under the
rose beds or under the herb garden,' Luke
said. He was sitting next to Madison, his
knee pressed against hers discreetly under
the table, his hand boldly on her den-
im-clad knee out of sight of the others.

Miranda nodded. 'It's possible, of
course; but then why add 'He tends them
all'? That has to be just as important.' She
templed her fingers over the painting.

'Cornelius must have meant the gardener. He'd be the only one who would tend the roses, box and herbs.' She stared at the rain-battered window, but they all knew that what she was really seeing were the gardens and grounds of Catesby Hall.

They exchanged nervous looks as the silence lengthened. Madison covered Luke's hand with her own. He immediately turned his over, linking his fingers through hers. They had barely managed a moment alone so far today. On waking, Madison had wondered if the wine and the excitement of finding the Spanish galleon had coloured her view of the previous evening. What if, when they met in the cold light of the next day, there was nothing there?

She needn't have worried. As soon as Luke opened the door of Rock Cottage to Madison and his mother, Madison had felt her heart pitter-patter down one side of her ribcage and then back up the other. His broad smile and quick, warm kiss to her cheek told her he felt the same, and she had walked on air into the kitchen.

Now, as the Professor cleared his throat, Miranda's reverie was broken, and she looked at each one of them in turn and smiled. Tapping the painting of the Spanish galleon on the table in front of her as if it were a good-luck talisman, she said, 'It's in the gardener's cottage, or under it.'

'The gardener's cottage?' Luke queried.

'When was it built?' the Professor asked.

'I always thought it was contemporaneous with the house,' Miranda said. 'But it could've been built in Cornelius Catesby's time. In his journal he talks about overseeing the construction of several outbuildings. I suppose one of those could have been the gardener's cottage.'

'Is anyone living there?' Madison asked.

'Gracious, no! The place is a ruin.' Miranda looked a little sheepish. 'I'm afraid I've rather let it go. As I understand it, the head gardener always lived there, and it was in continuous use from the time it was built right up until the First

World War. When most of the gardening team signed up to fight the Germans, the women of the village took over, and a lot of the gardens were turned over to the growing of vegetables. But as our head gardener at the time wasn't married, no one actually lived in the cottage. I think my grandfather always hoped the gardener would come home. Unfortunately, he was one of many who died in the awful fighting at the Somme.

'After the war, my grandfather employed a new head gardener, but he already had a cottage in the village where he and his family lived, and he had no wish to up sticks and move. Consequently, the gardener's cottage became outdated and forlorn. Successive gardeners eschewed it for smarter homes in the village.

'When my brother and I were children, we played inside it. It's been at the back of my mind to do something about it for years,' Miranda confessed. 'I've toyed with the idea of flattening it, but sentimentality has always held me back. I settled on the idea of renovating it and turning it into a holiday home, but it would be an expensive job, and somehow I've never got round to organising it.'

'So there's a pretty good chance that the fabric of the building's been undisturbed for years,' Luke said, edging forward.

Miranda nodded.

'And, at its heart, the original walls and floors are still there?' he queried.

'Yes,' Miranda confirmed. 'At least, I think so. I'd have to check the plans in the title deeds to be sure.'

'I think the time has come to talk to the police, Miranda,' the Professor said.

'I agree,' Luke chimed in. 'For one thing, we'll never be able to explore the gardener's cottage without Catesby or one of his men seeing us. We need him off our backs. And he should be in jail anyway for what he did to you and Madison,' he added.

Madison felt the pressure of Luke's fingers squeezing hers. Miranda gave her a sympathetic smile. 'I'd feel happier if we checked inside the gardener's cottage before we move against Teddy.'

'Why?' Luke asked, mystified.

'He's been ripping my house apart for weeks, Luke,' Miranda said, the shadow of anger darkening her eyes. 'What if he found another clue? Maybe the gardener's cottage just leads us on to another location.'

'More reason to get him out of the way,' Luke responded.

'He's my flesh and blood, Luke,' Miranda said, anguished. 'I might hate him with every fibre of my being right now, but I loved his father, my brother. My lawyer is in the process of drawing up a new will for me, and has written to the Office of the Public Guardian to stop Teddy registering the power of attorney he forged in his favour.'

'You don't want to go to the police?' Luke said, astonished. 'After everything he did to you?'

'He's a weak, misguided man. But now that we have the upper hand, I'd like to give him one more chance. You think me foolish, I know. I can see it on all of your faces. But just think, if it were one of your relatives, what would you do?'

'So we wait until your lawyer has all the paperwork in order?' Luke said, clearly frustrated. 'How long is that going to take?'

'My lawyer assures me that the paperwork will be ready tomorrow. Then he and I are going to Catesby Hall to have it out with Teddy face to face. I'll offer him the chance of an honourable retreat and then set about repairing all the damage he's done.'

'And if he doesn't take it?' Luke asked.

'Then he'll leave me with no choice but to bring in the police. For my brother's sake, I'd like to give him one last chance.'

One by one, they nodded. It was Miranda's house; Miranda's nephew. She had suffered more at his hand than anyone else. It was her choice.

'That doesn't mean, of course, that we can't investigate the gardener's cottage today,' Miranda added. 'If all it does is lead to another clue, I'd like to know as soon as possible, but we need the key.'

'I'll just smash a window or bust open

a door,' Luke said. 'If it's in as bad a state as you say, it won't be that difficult.'

'We can't leave any trace, Luke,' Miranda said sharply. 'If Teddy or his men spot a broken window or an open door, they'll know someone's been there and wonder why.'

'Wouldn't it just be better to wait twenty-four hours?' Kathryn suggested, her face tense.

Miranda, the Professor, Madison and Luke exchanged looks. They all knew it would be sensible to wait, but that it would be next to impossible for them to actually do it.

'I might as well be talking to myself,' Kathryn tutted.

'Where's the key?' the Professor asked.

'In the kitchen,' Miranda replied. 'First drawer beside the door. All the keys are there. It's a heavy, ornate key with an old paper label attached to it with string.'

Luke stroked his chin. 'So I'd need to slip into the house, and then —'

'No,' Kathryn cried out. 'Look at your face! My heart couldn't take it, Luke. It simply couldn't,' she declared.

'Ma, there's nothing wrong with your heart,' Luke replied.

'There soon will be,' she responded. 'What with all this stress!'

'I'll get the key,' Madison said quietly.

'What?' Luke turned to her. 'No!'

'So it's okay for you to risk it, but not for me?' she asked.

'Yes. No. I don't think it's a good idea,' he finished feebly.

'I could ring them,' Madison offered, 'and say I have some news from my grandfather; inveigle my way into the kitchen that way.'

'Bad idea, Stick,' the Professor said gently. 'Catesby's already proved he's a ruthless man.'

'Good — that's settled then,' Luke said firmly. 'I'll go up to the gardener's cottage and smash one of the back windows. We'd have to be incredibly unlucky for one of Catesby's thugs to spot that before you lawyer up tomorrow,' he added, looking at Miranda.

'Very well. I'll come with you,' she said.

'I'm sure I can manage,' Luke insisted gently.

'I'm sure you can, Luke. But it's my land. You'll not stop me,' she said firmly.

Luke made as if to argue.

'Remember all those times I caught you scrumping apples in my orchard?' Miranda said. 'I always pretended to look the other way. You owe me.'

Luke rubbed the back of his neck. 'Okay,' he said.

'I'm coming too,' Madison declared.

'Wait a minute, Maddy,' Luke said. 'It's going to be hard enough with two people sneaking up there, but three? We'll be inviting trouble. If I go with Miranda, we might just pull it off.'

Miranda traced her fingers over the scratches on the wooden frame. 'I don't want anyone else to get hurt,' she said quietly, catching Kathryn's look from across the table. 'Maybe it would be better to wait until tomorrow.'

'An outbreak of common sense! Hallelujah!' Kathryn said. 'Right. Now that's settled, if you'll all excuse me, I need to get back to my day job. And no, I don't need you to walk me back.' She stroked Luke's cheek.

'It's for the best,' the Professor confirmed, his hand over Miranda's.

Miranda nodded. 'I've waited all these years, so I suppose another twenty-four hours won't make much difference,' she said, sounding unconvinced.

'In the meantime, why don't I give the Spanish galleon a bit of a clean-up, restore her to some of her former glory?' Luke suggested.

Miranda brightened. 'I'd dearly love to see that. And while you're busy upstairs, I'll go through the deeds to the house my lawyer delivered yesterday afternoon. I want to be absolutely certain the gardener's cottage has always been on the same site. Madison, would you be a dear and help me go through the plans?'

Hoping she might have been able to join Luke in his studio, Madison quickly hid her disappointment. 'Yes of course,' she said with a smile.

Luke stood back from the painting of the Spanish galleon and appraised his work. A bit more definition was needed on the left-hand side, he decided.

'Permission to disturb the maestro at work?' Madison asked as she came up the spiral staircase from the second-floor landing.

Luke grinned and laid down his paint-brush. 'Permission granted,' he said. 'I need a break.'

He circled her waist with his arms and leaned in to kiss her lips. To his delight and relief, Madison was as warm and soft and welcoming as she had been the previous evening. He'd been plagued by doubts that morning, worried that the wine and the circumstances had led her to move too quickly and that she would attempt to row back. As soon as he saw her, however, his fears had been dispelled. Her sunny smile and quick catch of his fingers as she walked into Rock Cottage told him all he needed to know.

He drew back, smiling down at her. She was dressed in cream cargo trousers and a burgundy T-shirt. Did this woman own any skirts or dresses? Maybe he'd buy her some, so keen was he to catch a glimpse of her legs.

'How's it going?' Madison asked, nodding towards the Spanish galleon set up on his easel.

'Slowly,' he admitted. 'Restoration isn't my strongest suit. I need to be careful to enhance what's already there and not embellish it. It's a fine line.'

Madison moved on from examining the Spanish galleon more closely to looking around the loft. 'So this is the studio.' She turned back to him with a smile.

'This is it.'

'The light up here is terrific.'

He nodded. 'Got to have good light.'

'I don't regret what happened last night.' She tossed the words casually over her shoulder. 'In case you were wondering,' she added.

'I'd kind of assumed that was the case, but it's nice to hear you say it.'

She fingered the edge of a half-finished canvas. 'I'm not sure where we go next.'

To bed, Luke thought, *with a bit of luck.* He held back the remark. He could see from the frown lines scoring her forehead that she didn't need a flippant response. What she needed was reassurance.

'Would you like me to tell you where I see us heading next?' he asked.

'Please.'

'While you and the Professor are still here in Penrowan, and once all this craziness is over —' He waved in the direction of the Spanish galleon. '— I'd like the opportunity to show you the Penrowan and the Cornwall I love.'

'That sounds nice.'

Encouraged, he continued, 'I see us building on our friendship and getting to know one another better, but taking things slowly. When you and the Prof head back to London, we can keep in touch by email and Skype. I can visit you there, you can visit me here. And when, or if, you're ready to move things to the next level, I'll be waiting. But I won't pressure you or hassle you. You've had a rough few months, and you need to move at a pace you feel comfortable with. I respect that.' He paused, keen to gauge her reaction.

Speech over, he watched, uncertain, as she stared out through the skylights over Penrowan Harbour. He'd said what he thought she wanted to hear, but that didn't make it any less true. He was willing to be patient. Madison was the kind of woman who was worth waiting for. Luke frowned. She still hadn't moved or said anything. He reviewed his speech. Was it too much? Did she not believe him?

'Madison?' He touched her elbow gently.

She turned to him, and it was then he saw the sheen of tears in her eyes. His heart dropped, so full was it with love for this woman. 'Please don't cry,' he said weakly.

'What you said was lovely. Have you been rehearsing that?'

'Maybe once or twice,' he admitted. 'But I meant every word,' he added quickly.

She smiled. 'When you asked me if I'd like you to tell me where you see us heading next, I half-expected you to say to bed,' she said with a giggle.

'Well that can be arranged too,' he replied smartly, then held up his hands. 'But seriously, it's your pace, your rules.'

She nodded. 'Thank you. I'm going to need some time.'

'Of course. I understand.'

He watched her take a deep breath and blow it out, her shoulders relaxing as she did so. 'Can I look around?'

'Sure. You might find that back corner interesting. It's where I keep all the storm paintings.'

He sat on the battered sofa, his ankle hooked over his knee, watching as she moved the canvases around, making appreciative noises as she looked at each one. He was gratified. She wasn't just flicking through them; she was really studying them. He could see the hard edge of concentration in her gaze. Every now and then she would throw him a look and smile.

When she'd got all the storm paintings out in the open, she stood in the middle of them, hands on hips. 'You do know these are extraordinary, don't you?' she said.

'I put a lot into them,' Luke said.

'I can tell. There's real passion here, rage and anger. Their rawness is mesmerising. I can hardly bring myself to look away,' she admitted.

Her words stirred Luke's soul. Whenever he completed one of his storm scenes, he always felt wrung out afterwards, because of the emotional intensity he poured into the work.

'Don't get me wrong; the sunny scenes are well-painted too. But these are on a different level. Why is that?'

Luke hesitated. To explain, he'd have to talk about the accident. Maybe Madison wasn't the only one who needed to take things slowly. He shrugged, and watched Madison's eyes narrow in response.

'Come on, Ryder! You don't get to

shrug me off. These are chalk and cheese. Why?'

Luke rubbed a hand over his chin. If it were time to trust again, he had to be prepared to put himself on the line. Holding back wouldn't cut it with someone as perceptive as Madison.

He stood, turning away from her penetrating gaze, and stared across the harbour to the opposite headland, seeking the outline of the telephone rock. 'There was an accident. My dad and my brother, Pete, were killed.' Somehow he managed to keep the emotion out of his voice. That was good. He didn't want her to think he was a wuss.

'I'm so sorry,' she said. 'What happened?'

Luke felt his insides twist at the sympathy in her voice. A matter-of-fact recounting of the events of that storm-tossed night he could just about manage, but too much emotion and he'd crack.

He kept his gaze fixed on the opposite headland. 'Dad and Pete were fishermen. They'd taken their boat out like they always did. It was blowing a gale, but that's not unusual for Cornwall in November. The forecast was bad, but they'd fished in worse.' His gaze tracked down the steep bank of the headland to the harbour and the pleasure boats pitching to and fro. 'The weather took an unexpected turn for the worse. They decided to head for home, but there was a problem with the engine. It was dark. It was cold. The weather was filthy. They radioed for help.' He sneaked a look over his shoulder. Madison was standing with her arms wrapped around her as if she was feeling the weather he was describing and hugging herself to ward off the cold.

He met her gaze and quickly looked away. The honesty in her face was too much; her eyes were large and luminous with tears. He turned abruptly and began to pace the studio. 'The Tregelian lifeboat launched, but by the time they reached the vessel, it was badly smashed up by the waves. They managed to attach a line, but there was no one on board. They searched the area, but there was no sign of Dad or

Pete. The boat sank thirty minutes later.'

'Oh Luke, how awful!'

He kept his head down and started to pace. *Get the rest of it out, and then the worst is done. Telling her about Georgie and Melissa will be a doddle after this.* 'I was in London in my second year at St Martins when it happened. I travelled back to Cornwall through the night.'

'Poor Kathryn. She must have been in pieces. You too, of course,' Madison added quickly. 'But your poor mother ...'

'It was tough on her. She comes from a fishing family, and we all know the risks — how capricious the sea can be; benign one minute, treacherous the next. But knowing the risk is one thing; confronting the reality is something else. She had to face up to the fact that her husband and her firstborn son were never coming home.'

He continued to pace. *Give her the last bit of information and then you're done.* He sucked in a breath, gathering his strength.

'Did they ever recover their bodies?'

Madison asked gently.

He stopped and nodded numbly. He was there again in that sanitised hospital room, a strong chemical smell in his nostrils, the white walls a stark backdrop to his red-hot pain. He could see once more the pretty Filipino nurse that attended him; could picture her black and red glasses, the sympathy in her eyes. He remembered the scar on the back of her left hand and her bright red nail polish. Every detail of her appearance was burned into his brain. It was as if she were in the room with him now, slowly folding back the sheet to reveal his father's battered face.

Luke cleared his throat, wiping the vision from his mind. 'If the tides and currents are right, a lot of debris ...' Jesus, had he really just used that word? 'Sometimes wreckage gets caught and lodged between the rocks on the far side of Tregelian. The wreckage from Dad's boat started to appear the next day; and then, on the next tide, more of it came ashore, along with Dad and Pete. I had to identify the bodies.'

Madison gasped. 'I can't imagine how dreadful that must have been for you.'

He hadn't even acknowledged he was crying until he felt Madison kiss his wet cheek and pull him into her arms. His own arms hung limply at his sides, and he willed himself to lift them, to hold her back. He felt her guide him backwards and down onto the sofa. He laid his cheek against her shoulder, her hair falling across his face. It felt so good to be held like that, her gentle fingers stroking his face and arm as he sobbed.

'Cry it out, darling,' she said softly, smoothing back his hair.

At last he was spent; there were no more tears and he felt inordinately tired, as drained as if he had just finished painting one of the big storm canvases. 'I've always felt guilty,' he admitted quietly. The words fell like stones into the silence; the rocks he had carried in his heart ever since it had happened.

'Why? There was nothing you could've done.'

'I should've been there, on the boat with them. Maybe the three of us could've saved her; saved each other. Instead I was gallivanting about in London.'

'I doubt very much if your presence on that boat could have changed the outcome, Luke. Mostly likely, the sea would've taken you, too.'

He felt her grip tighten at her last words. Hers was the voice of common sense, he knew, but common sense didn't hold a lot of sway at two o'clock in the morning when you were alone in bed listening to a howling sou'westerly and trying to imagine what those last panic-filled moments must have been like for them and then trying just as earnestly to forget.

'You need to let go of the guilt,' Madison said softly. 'Your dad and your brother wouldn't want you to torture yourself like that. I bet they were both proud of you for winning a place at St Martins, weren't they?'

He nodded as he straightened up, rubbing his hands over his eyes. 'Sorry, really didn't want to make an idiot of myself.'

He pushed his hands through his hair.

'You didn't,' Madison said swiftly. 'You've been carrying these feelings of guilt around a long time. Too long.' She stroked his cheek. 'It's time to let them go, don't you think?'

The feelings, or Dad and Pete? All of it, probably, the feelings and them. Leaning forward, elbows on his knees, Luke stared at the paint-spattered floor.

'That's why you never went back, isn't it?' Madison asked gently.

'I couldn't. Mum fell apart. She needed me to be here for her. If I hadn't stayed, she'd have lost the business and her home. For the first two years I kept the B&B afloat, and then gradually she started to do more, to rediscover her spark. The insurance money came through, and Mum bought this place as somewhere for her to retire when she couldn't look after Harbour Watch anymore. Until then, she was happy for me to rent it from her.'

'Didn't you have the option of deferring your studies?' Madison asked. 'Surely, given the circumstances, that would've been possible?'

'I didn't ask. By the time Mum was anywhere near back to her old self, three years had gone by, and I'd made a life for myself back here. Georgie and I were divorced, and...'

'Whoa! Back up. Georgie?'

He rubbed a hand on the back of his neck. Poor, sweet, young Georgie. 'We were nineteen when we married, kids playing at being adults. Everyone said don't do it.' He shrugged. 'You don't listen at that age. If anything, it spurred us on. Georgie was a Londoner. I met her at St Martins. She came down to Cornwall with me for a bit after the accident. Then she went back to school. We'd hook up at the holidays.'

'That must have been tough.'

'You never know how strong a relationship is until it's been tested. Ours turned out to be not very strong at all. Georgie was a city girl. The thought of burying herself in Cornwall — I think she actually used that phrase ... well, let's just say it was never going to happen. I had obligations here. I couldn't up and leave even if I wanted to, and after what had happened to Dad and Pete, I didn't want to. I felt I owed it to them to stay and see Ma right.'

'You did a brave thing.'

Luke snorted and shook his head. 'Going out on a boat to earn a living from the sea in a bad storm is brave. What I did is what any good son should do.'

'So you and Georgie divorced?' Madison prompted.

'Yeah. We limped on for a couple of years and then called it a day.'

Standing, Luke indicated the beach scenes and summer landscapes leaning against the wall. 'You asked why the paintings were so different,' he said. 'These I paint with my head and a little bit of my soul.' Next he pointed at the stormscapes, 'These I paint with a broken heart and all of my soul.'

Madison stood and, looping her arm around his waist, rested her head on his shoulder. Luke hugged her back, liking the feel of her close to him. They fitted together well.

'You punish yourself by reliving it, don't you?' Madison said gently.

'I suppose I do.' He'd never thought about it like that before. It was just a need, a drive to pour his feelings out onto the canvas; and each time, when it was done, he slept twelve hours straight.

'Do you still want one?' He cocked an eyebrow as he looked down at her.

'You bet.' She pointed. 'That one.'

He followed her finger to a painting of Penrowan Point under siege from sea and sky. 'Storm at the Headland?'

'Is that what it's called?'

He grinned. 'It's a painting of a storm battering Penrowan Point. You'll find I don't go in for flowery titles.'

She grinned back at him. 'How much is it?'

'I'm not selling it to you,' he said, stung even by the suggestion. 'It's yours.'

'Luke ...'

'My apology for making a fool of you on the telephone rock.'

He looked with fresh eyes at the

canvas. The sky was a purple bruise of laden storm clouds, the grey sea a broiling mass. Black rocks, jagged and terrifying, were being swamped by foamy spray. Overhead, one lonely seagull was buffeted by the gale as it flew above the maelstrom.

Luke nodded to himself as if satisfied. It was one of his better ones. 'I'll parcel it up, ready for you to take home with you,' he said.

The words seemed to drop into a chasm between them. Neither of them wanted to contemplate her leaving.

Madison linked her fingers through his. 'Tell me about wife number two,' she said quietly.

Oh, Jesus! He felt the pressure of her fingers increase. She wasn't going to let him get away with brushing her off like he'd done last night. He felt a bit of a heel about that anyway. She had been brave enough to talk about her marriage, and then when she'd opened the door for him to talk about his, he'd slammed it firmly shut in her face. She looked up at him, her eyebrows lifting in two perfect arches.

'She was a local girl called Melissa. Family had been in Tregelian for generations. I guess, in the end, I didn't give her enough attention.' Luke sighed, remembering the rows. 'She wanted me to stop painting,' he said finally.

'What?' Madison cried, turning to him. 'Why?'

'She resented the hours I spent up here. She didn't like the person I was when I was painting a storm canvas. Some of the big ones can take weeks, and I can get a bit...' He searched for the right word. 'Obsessed with it,' he said, finally. 'Then, when it's finished, I collapse and sleep round the clock.

'I should have known the marriage was in real trouble when she stopped complaining about my painting, but I didn't pick up on it. I carried on regardless, relishing the outbreak of peace.' He gave an ironic laugh. 'Turns out she was having an affair.' The muscles in his cheek clenched. 'It might not have been so bad, I might even have been able to forgive her, but the man she had the affair with was Teddy Catesby.'

'What?' Madison cried, astonished.

'She knew we hated each other; had done since we were children. I think that was part of the attraction for her.'

Madison's hands were on his shoulders, her soft fingers massaging his skin. 'That was a horrible thing to do to you. How did you find out?'

'I was doing some work for Mick up by the station. I was finishing up, about to walk home, when I saw Catesby's car pull up in the station car park. There was a woman in the passenger seat; I couldn't see her clearly. What I could see was the passionate kiss they exchanged.' Luke gave a mirthless laugh. 'I remember thinking, poor woman, she doesn't have any idea what she's getting herself into. Then the poor woman got out of the car, still exchanging sweet nothings with her lover, and I realised it was my wife.'

'I'm so sorry, Luke.'

'I confronted them and dragged Catesby out of the car. Melissa was begging me not to hit him. It'd been going on for four months. She said she loved him. I went home alone and she spent the night at Catesby Hall. The next day she came to get her stuff.'

Madison's lips were a soft balm to his cheek and then his mouth. 'Is she still with him now?'

'No. It fizzled out a couple of months after our divorce came through. I think she was putting pressure on him to marry her and Catesby ran for the hills. I don't think he ever really loved her. I think he just loved punishing me.'

'Do you still see her?'

He caught the slight inflection in her tone and cupped his hand to her cheek. 'She lives in Tregelian with her second husband and a baby daughter. I see her occasionally in the street or in a pub. We're civil to one another but that's about it. There's no attraction left.'

'No, betrayal kills it stone dead, doesn't it?' Madison mused.

'Sure does,' he agreed. He stroked her cheek. 'I'm used goods, Maddy,' Luke said. 'I have issues.' He indicated the storm canvases.

Madison smiled and kissed his lips. 'Good. I hate boring men.'

'Madison! Madison!' They turned at the sound of the Professor's voice. 'Luke? Madison?'

They both hurried down the spiral staircase from the attic. Madison's heart was in her mouth. Registering her grandfather's panicked tone, she half-expected to find him on the floor after a fall. Instead, she almost ran into him on the landing, with Luke nearly colliding with her back so suddenly had she stopped. 'Are you okay? What's wrong?'

'It's Miranda. She's gone to the Hall.'

'What?' Madison and Luke exclaimed together.

'I went into the kitchen to read through some of my papers while Madison and Miranda went over the plans and deeds of Catesby Hall. When I came through to see if anyone wanted a cup of tea, the lounge was empty. I found this note pinned beneath the mermaid sculpture on the fireplace.'

Madison took the note and held it so that both she and Luke could read it.

I'm sorry. I've waited a lifetime to find the treasure belonging to the Spanish galleon. Now that we're within touching distance, I can't stand the thought of waiting another twenty-four hours. I just want to make sure the fabric of the gardener's cottage is still intact. I'll be fine. Please DON'T come after me.

Madison turned to look at Luke.

'Well, we'll have to go after her, obviously,' Luke said. 'I bet she's used the smugglers' tunnel. Of course, we have no idea how much of a head start she had on us. Did you pinpoint the location of the gardener's cottage?'

Madison nodded. 'It's in a little glade to the right of the main house. I'll show you on the plans.'

'So it's sheltered from sight from the main house?'

'Yes,' Madison confirmed.

They went downstairs and she laid out

one of the plans. 'Here's Catesby Hall,' she said, pointing. 'And here's the cottage.'

Luke studied the plan, his brows drawn together in concentration. 'Right,' he said. 'I'll get going.'

'I'll come with you,' Madison said.

'No!' Her grandfather and Luke spoke in unison.

She stared at them both, a steely look in her eye. 'You don't expect me to sit and wait here?' she said, outraged at the thought.

'Like I said to Miranda before, it's going to be tough enough for two people to run through the grounds of the Hall and not be spotted. Three people is just inviting trouble — and I think we've got enough of that already, don't you?'

'Quite right,' her grandfather chipped in.

Madison scowled. She was outnumbered, and what they said made sense, but she couldn't stand the thought of doing nothing while Luke potentially put himself in harm's way.

'Why couldn't Miranda have waited?'

she said angrily.

'Because she's a stubborn woman who has spent her life chasing after a dream,' her grandfather replied. 'Could any of us, hand on heart, withstand the temptation if we were in her shoes?'

Luke was already heading to the door. 'I'll be back with Miranda as soon as I can. Please don't tell my mother where I've gone if you can possibly help it.'

'Wait!' Madison called. 'At least let me walk with you up to Bill Warren's place.'

Luke shrugged. 'Okay.'

He kept up a steady pace through the steeply winding streets that led to Bill Warren's cottage. Madison had to trot to keep up with him.

'Please be careful,' she said as they reached Bill's front gate. Catching hold of him, she brought Luke into her arms. Fuelled by fear and adrenaline, her kiss was passionate.

'Maybe I'll leave Miranda to fend for herself,' Luke joked.

Madison slapped his arm playfully.

'I'll see you soon, Maddy.'

Bill opened his front window.

'Sorry about this, Bill.'

'No problem, lad. Said you could all come and go as many times as you wanted. I ain't got no use for no old tunnel.' He grinned a toothless grin.

'How long ago did Miranda come through?' Luke asked, looking tense.

'I'd say half an hour or so.'

She'd be through the tunnel and into the garden by now. Madison met Luke's gaze, knowing he was making the same calculation.

'I'd better get a move on then,' he said. He jogged up the steep incline of Bill's back garden. Halfway he stopped and turned. 'You've not got some crazy idea about following me, have you?' Luke asked Madison.

She shook her head. 'The thought never entered my mind.'

He nodded, satisfied, and blew her a kiss.

As soon as he was out of sight, Madison gave Bill a cheery wave and headed back to the village at a run. She had no intention of following Luke into that pitch-black tunnel, but she did have another crazy idea in mind.

12

Luke scrambled through the smugglers' tunnel as quickly as he dared. He'd been playing in these tunnels since he was a nipper, but after rainfall the rock was always slick with the runoff, making the floor slippery. One wrong move and he could lose his footing and bang his head. He'd be no use to anyone unconscious, so he took care to moderate his pace.

He silently berated himself. He'd left in such haste that he'd forgotten to pick up a torch. To take his mind off the suffocating darkness, he thought about Madison's parting kiss; how sweet her lips had felt against his. He hoped she'd keep her word about not following him. He knew he'd have his work cut out spiriting Miranda away unseen, and he didn't fancy his chances if all three of them had to make a getaway. There was no boat this time to speed their flight.

Soon he was at the fork in the tunnel. He could hear the sea whooshing and roaring along the narrow stretch to his left, driven in by the high wind and spring tide, but he quickly turned to his right. He had been through the tunnels without a torch before, using touch to get him through, but it was a slow process. In his mind's eye he conjured up the outline of the tunnel, the jagged pieces of rock sticking out to catch some poor person unawares. He'd taken one knock to the elbow when his concentration faltered, but all in all he figured he'd made good time.

He crouched in the entrance to the tunnel and surveyed the orchard. It seemed quiet. He closed his eyes and thought about the plan he'd studied before leaving home. He had to go to his left across the orchard, skirt around the formal lawn and into the thicket of trees that ran along its far edge. He then had to go through the thicket to emerge in the glade where the gardener's cottage was located.

There was a lot that could go wrong. The formal lawn worried him, as he would be at his most exposed there. The thicket of trees, while extending him ample cover, also presented a problem. What if he lost his bearings and exited at the wrong point, missing the glade altogether, and blundered into Catesby or his men?

To be honest, it all worried him. *Counter-productive, Luke! You're here now, and at least it's stopped raining. What's the worst that could happen? Muscles might hit you again.* Actually, that was pretty bad. He'd been lucky the guy hadn't shattered his cheekbone last time. He'd had the feeling the man had held back a little weight from the punch. That wouldn't happen if he was caught on Catesby land again.

He shook his head at his own negativity and checked the orchard once more. The place didn't seem to be in an uproar, which would suggest that Miranda had not been apprehended. Surely she couldn't have got so much of a head start on him that she'd made it to the garden, been caught and bundled off, all before he got here. Then again, she'd probably remembered to bring a torch. He scoffed once more at his oversight and loped across the orchard, keeping low, waiting to hear a shout at any moment.

He made it to the beech hedging that ran around the back of the orchard. A gap had been cut so people could move from the formal lawn into the orchard and back again. The main house was now to his right. He chanced a look round the hedge.

The formal lawn had been mown in perfect stripes. There was a slight incline leading up to the house, but just to the left of where Luke stood, the ground fell away into a rampant herbaceous border. He didn't fancy his chances running across open ground. It would be too easy to spot him from the house. He studied the border. Huge rhododendrons stood guardian along it, their deep green, waxy leaves waving in a suddenly sharp breeze. Luke could taste the tang of salt in the air.

Ducking back into the orchard, he looked along the beech hedge to the far end of the orchard. There was another gap in the hedge there. He jogged along to it. Ahead of him was a long, thin, grassy path lined on each side by the skeletal branches of ancient yews. So tightly woven were the branches of the yew tunnel that much of the daylight failed to penetrate, giving the walkway a mysterious twilight feel. The yew tunnel ran the length of the herbaceous border. It was by far the better option. Luke knew he could pass unseen from the house and reach the relative safety of the thicket of trees if he ran along it. He only had to hope that he didn't meet one of Catesby's men — or Catesby himself — coming back the opposite way, because once in the yew tunnel, there was absolutely nowhere to hide and no chance to retrace his steps undetected.

Throwing himself forward before he could change his mind, Luke ran as fast as he could along the pathway, praying the whole time no one would suddenly appear at the far end. As he neared the end of the tunnel, he moderated his pace and paused to catch his breath. So far, so good.

His heart pounded in his chest as he ducked his head for a quick look. There was a neat concrete path leading down from the house and away to his left. Beyond it was a scrubby piece of grass, and then beyond that the thicket of trees he was aiming for.

He caught a flash of movement in the trees and shrank back. Crouching down, he melted into the gloom of the tunnel. When he looked back, he saw Miranda emerge from the thicket and sprint, gazelle-like, to a tumbledown ruin to his left. Not waiting to question why she was running *away* from the gardener's cottage, Luke took off after her.

The tumbledown building had two and a half walls and no roof that Luke could make out. With a glance over his shoulder, he ran inside, only just avoiding the lump of wood that came soaring towards his head. Despite his quick parry to the left, Miranda still managed to land a resounding blow on his shoulder, making him stagger and nearly lose his footing.

'Luke?' Miranda whispered in horror. 'I'm so sorry. I thought you were one of them!' She let the piece of wood fall to the floor and quickly put her hand on his back. 'Are you okay?'

Luke straightened up. His shoulder hurt like mad, but he wasn't about to admit it. He sucked in a breath and blew it out slowly. 'Bit winded,' he said quietly. 'I'll be fine. Have you been spotted?' he asked, looking over his shoulder once more.

'Don't think so. There's two of them circling the grounds. I didn't want to risk crossing the thicket. It's too easy to give yourself away in the undergrowth. I thought I'd wait it out in here until they'd finished this section and headed back to the house. I doubt very much if they'll come this way, so we should be safe.'

Surreptitiously, Luke gave his shoulder a rub. 'What is this place?'

'The folly. Built as a romantic ruin by Milton Catesby. The Victorians were very much into their follies and grottoes.' She gave Luke a searching look. 'You didn't have to come after me, you know. The last thing I wanted was for anyone else to put themselves in harm's way.'

'If you thought I could sit at home knowing where you were and what you were doing, you don't know me very well, Miranda.'

She squeezed his arm as a frown grazed her forehead. 'Kathryn will kill me if anything happens to you.'

'Probably,' Luke replied amiably. 'So we'd better make sure nothing does,' he added with a smile. He chanced a look out of the glassless aperture of the folly and quickly ducked. He motioned for Miranda to join him in the darkest corner.

He could hear two sets of footsteps walking slowly, and a snatch of conversation about a boxing match. The footsteps faded, but Luke could still hear the conversation. Presumably the two men had stepped onto the grass, thereby softening their footfalls. Eventually their voices faded away.

Luke motioned for Miranda to remain in the folly. Heading out, he quickly spotted the two men moving in the direction of the orchard. He returned to Miranda.

'They're almost at the orchard. Let's give them a couple of minutes, and then I reckon it'll be safe to head off.'

She nodded. 'May I be so bold as to ask how things are between you and Madison?'

Luke smiled. 'Madison and I are getting on very well, thank you.'

Her lips twitched into a smile. 'I'm glad. It was obvious how she felt about you when you rescued us in your boat the other night. I'm not sure she'd even acknowledged it to herself at that stage, but I could tell just from the way she was looking at you.'

Luke raised an eyebrow in surprise. He had been too busy guiding the boat through the choppy waters to notice Madison looking at him at all, let alone in a way that may have betrayed her inner feelings about him. As he recalled, when they had reached Rock Cottage and climbed up from the boat to the deck, she had been in combative mood as he'd fished for compliments. It must have been her defence mechanism kicking in, he realised. Far easier to deny any attraction and hold him at arm's length by constantly jousting with him, than risk lowering her guard and making herself vulnerable.

If it hadn't been for the thrill and excitement of uncovering the Spanish galleon, would they ever have forged a way across the chasm that had separated them? He seriously doubted it. Reason enough to be grateful to the graceful old ship, he decided, whether or not they succeeded in recovering her treasure.

'Shall we go and find my inheritance?' Miranda asked.

Luke nodded. Catching the anticipation in her voice, he couldn't help but admire her tenacity. While he was annoyed they were taking a risk which for the sake of another twenty-four hours they needn't have taken, he could understand the passion driving her on.

As they made their way across to the thicket of trees and through them, Luke noticed that Miranda was carrying herself better than the night of her rescue. She was standing taller now, her shoulders back proudly. She even looked younger. It was amazing what proper rest, his mother's home cooking, and the lure of a centuries-old puzzle could achieve. Miranda Catesby was a new woman.

It took five minutes to cross the thicket. The glade looked serene. At the far end the cottage sat, squat and neglected, aglow in the early-evening sunshine.

'Is there a back door?' Luke asked. Miranda nodded.

They circled round and approached the cottage from behind. Miranda tried the handle. Luke also tried it in case the wood was warped and stuck, but it would not budge.

Cupping her hands around her eyes, Miranda peered through the dusty window to the side of the door. 'I think the key's in the lock on the other side,' she said, looking back at Luke. 'They must've checked the cottage after I escaped and left the key behind.'

'I can break a pane of glass, reach in and turn the key,' he suggested. 'I doubt Catesby's men would be so thorough as to check the back of the cottage.'

She nodded. 'Go ahead.'

'May I borrow your coat, Miranda?'

She quickly took it off and handed it to him. He wrapped it around his elbow. 'Turn away,' he said. When she had done so, he turned his face and brought his elbow back sharp and hard against the glass. The pane splintered, falling onto the wooden floor inside. With his elbow still covered, he pushed in the remaining jagged pieces before carefully shaking out Miranda's coat and handing it back to her. Then, reaching inside, he felt along the door until he found the lock and finally the key. Arching his wrist, he turned it. Miranda was waiting to try the handle. The door opened easily.

'We're in!' Miranda exclaimed, a delighted smile on her face.

The cottage was in a poor state of

repair, with wallpaper hanging from the walls and a strong smell of damp.

'I should never have let it get so bad,' she said, shaking her head. 'It's okay to be nostalgic about one's youth, but buildings need light and heat and people. When this is over, I'll give this cottage the facelift it deserves.'

'Hopefully when this is over, you'll have the funds to do it with,' Luke said with a grin. 'Where do we start?'

'The journal entry read NW six paces, EW three paces. I think NW is north wall.'

Luke nodded as he kicked the broken glass out of sight behind a piece of faded carpet. 'Right. So EW must be east wall.'

'That's what I think,' Miranda confirmed. 'This is the north wall.' She stood against it, pressing her hands flat against the tattered floral wallpaper. 'And that's the eastern one.' She pointed to it.

Luke moved across to the eastern wall. 'Take six good paces. Let's see where we finish up.'

Miranda paced, counting as she did so.

Luke moved along the eastern wall and took three paces into the room towards Miranda. 'The intersection of the two points is here,' he said, crouching down. 'I suppose it's too much to hope that an X marks the spot.'

Miranda laughed. 'That would be too easy.'

'I'll roll this rug back and see what's underneath. Just keep a check out the front, will you? I don't want one of Catesby's men surprising us.'

Miranda marked the spot on the floor with an old oil lamp before positioning herself beside the front window. 'All clear,' she said.

Luke rolled up the rug, coughing as decades of dust billowed up. He stared at the wide wooden floorboards beneath. 'I'm no expert, but these look original,' he said.

Miranda crouched beside him. 'They match some of the floorboards in the house,' she confirmed.

'We need to lever this one up. I don't suppose you keep any tools here?'

'There was a box of tools that belonged to the last gardener. They're bound to be in a bit of a state, but they were kept next door.'

The box was full of museum pieces so far as Luke was concerned, but there was a crowbar. It was covered in cobwebs and a little rusty in places, but it seemed robust enough to do the job.

He returned to the main room and traced the floorboard along until he found a join. 'I'm going to ruin your lovely floor, Miranda,' he warned.

'You have my permission.'

It was hard to work the end of the crowbar into the narrow join and get any purchase. It took several minutes of fiddling and swearing under his breath before Luke had finally got the end of the crowbar down far enough to attempt any sort of lift. The old wooden plank groaned as Luke put his back into it.

'Sounds almost human,' Miranda remarked.

At last the floorboard began to lift. From somewhere along its length there was a sharp crack, and the last third of the board sheared off completely, revealing a narrow opening.

'Hand me your torch, Miranda,' Luke said.

She did as she was asked. Luke lay down on the floor, angling the torch into the dark cavity beneath the floorboards and straining to see what, if anything, was down there.

'What can you see?' Miranda cried excitedly.

'Not much — the floor joists and the earthen floor beneath that. Wait!' He shifted position. With his gaze firmly fixed on the hole in the floor, he reached for the crowbar and manoeuvred it beneath the floorboards.

'What is it?'

Sitting up, he brushed the dust off himself. 'Did those plans of yours say anything about a well?'

'A well? Under the cottage? No. There was an old well in the back garden.'

'Looks as though under the very spot you marked is an old well. It's been capped with a wooden top. Looks as though it's made from the same wood as the floorboards.'

'So they capped the well and then constructed the floor over the top of it?'

Luke nodded. 'Not sure why you'd do that with a perfectly useful well unless you had something other than water in it.'

'You think Cornelius stored the treasure in the original well and then built the cottage over the top, before sinking a new well in the back garden?'

'Could be.'

'In which case, there must've been an even older dwelling on this site that predates all the plans I have.'

'Even if I lifted the rest of the floorboards and managed to get the cap off the well, we'd need specialist equipment to lift anything that's down there. As frustrating as it is, Miranda, I think we've come to the end of the road for today.'

'I agree.' She clutched Luke's arm. 'This floor hasn't been touched in centuries, Luke. You do realise what this means, don't you?' Her eyes were aglow with excitement, the years positively falling away from her.

Luke nodded. 'I'd say there's a fairly good chance that the Spanish galleon's treasure, or at least Cornelius's share of it, is still down there.' Standing, he brought Miranda into his arms and hugged her. 'I'm delighted for you, Miranda. Really, I am. You've waited a long time for this.'

'A lifetime,' she said breathlessly. 'And if it is there, we'll all share in my good fortune. I can promise you that.'

'We've got to get at it first. Reckon we're going to need a winch; and if we don't want to do the whole thing by hand, we're going to need a generator too.' She nodded. 'I'll speak to a couple of people in the village; call in some favours. In the meantime, I'll pop this board back and cover it over. It'll be good enough to fool anyone who looks in the window or opens the front door. So long as they don't tread on the exact spot, we should be fine.'

'Even if they do, they'll probably just think it's rotten,' Miranda said.

Luke returned the crowbar to the box

of tools in the room next door. As he did so, a movement at the edge of the glade caught his eye. Two men were ambling across, heading directly for the cottage. Luke froze. Were they safer outside the cottage or inside? Taking a split-second decision, he decided outside gave them more options. Returning to the main room, he put his finger to his lips and motioned for Miranda to join him.

'Two men coming to the cottage,' he whispered. 'Let's get outside.'

They slipped silently out the back door. Luke could hear the men talking. A moment later, he smelled cigarette smoke. He mimicked a man smoking and Miranda nodded. Holding himself taut, Luke knew they had no option but to wait until the two men had finished their break and had gone on their way. Straining to listen, he heard a radio crackle into life.

'Robbo, where are you?'

One of the men swore, clearly not happy about having his break interrupted. 'Gardener's cottage.'

'Is Pav with you?'

'Yes. What do you want?'

'Boss has a visitor. He wants everyone back at the house now for a briefing.'

'Okay.'

Luke exchanged glances with Miranda, who nodded, confirming she had heard. The two men moved off, their voices growing fainter. Luke chanced a look round the edge of the cottage. The men were on the far side of the glade now and didn't look back.

'If they're pulling everyone back to the house, it'll give us a chance to get away, but we can't hang around,' Luke said.

Miranda nodded. 'I wonder who the visitor is?' she mused as they ran through the thicket of trees, heading back the way they had come.

'Whoever it is, I'm grateful to them,' Luke said. *Understatement of the year,* he thought. A clear run through to the tunnel and out the other side was beyond his wildest dreams. Someone was looking after them.

Although they were cautious, the garden was clear, and they were soon back at the tunnel. Buoyed by their recent discovery, their minds full of what the morning would bring, they made short work of negotiating its narrow twists and turns. Eager to share the good news with Madison, Kathryn and the Professor, they walked at a brisk pace from Bill Warren's garden to Rock Cottage.

Luke thrust open the door to his home and stepped back to allow Miranda to enter. They were greeted by the anxious faces of his mother and the Professor.

'Is everything okay?' Kathryn asked.

'Couldn't be better, Ma,' Luke said jovially. Then he paused. 'Where's Maddy?'

'We thought she was with you,' the Professor said. 'Isn't she?' he asked hopefully.

'No, I thought she was coming back here to wait with you.'

The Professor shook his head. 'She never came back.'

A cold hand seized Luke's heart as his gaze met Miranda's. Had Catesby's visitor been Madison?

13

Madison Morley gulped at the glass of flavoured water Teddy Catesby had given her and tried to pretend she wasn't nervous. What had seemed like a good idea in the safety of the bustling Penrowan harbour seemed less appealing the longer she sat in the library at Catesby Hall.

She reminded herself about what had driven her here in the first place: the thought of Luke being assaulted by Catesby's men and Miranda being snatched once more. She had figured that her presence would at the very least create some confusion in Catesby's mind and act as a diversionary tactic, making it easier for Luke and Miranda to get back to the village. When Catesby disappeared shortly after her arrival, it had seemed as though the plan was paying off, because Madison was sure she had spied Muscles and another man crossing the lawn and heading back to the house.

She took a nonchalant sip of her water. She was standing in front of an impressive wall of old books and turned as Catesby entered. 'What a beautiful library,' she said with what she hoped was a winning smile.

'Yes, we're very lucky. I'm sorry I had to step out. Please forgive me, but I may have to do so again shortly.'

'That's fine. I should've called first. If this is a bad time, I can always come back.' With her objective of creating a diversion working even better than she had hoped, Madison could think of nothing better than escaping Catesby Hall and heading back to the village … and Luke.

'Nonsense,' Teddy Catesby said smoothly. 'Delighted to have your company. Please sit down.'

Madison sat at one end of a large sage-green Chesterfield.

'You were telling me about your grandfather,' Catesby prompted.

'Oh, yes. He rang to say he's finished his business in Oxford and will be coming down to Penrowan tomorrow. I told him about Miranda's disappearance and he was very concerned. Unfortunately he hasn't seen or heard from her, but he's keen to do everything he can to help. I'm expecting him on the four o'clock train, and he's hoping to come and meet with you tomorrow evening to talk about what's happened and see what he can do to assist.'

She'd been rehearsing the speech in the taxi all the way from the village to the imposing front door of Catesby Hall. She'd been careful to maintain eye contact throughout and hold her glass very still. Had she done enough to fool him?

Catesby strode to the window and stood looking out, tapping his finger against the leaded glass. 'That's very good of him. Tomorrow evening, you say?'

Madison nodded. 'That's what he suggested.' She stood her glass down on a coaster on the occasional table at her side. 'I take it you haven't heard from your aunt?'

Catesby shook his head. 'Sadly, no.'

Madison turned as the door to the library opened and Muscles appeared. Involuntarily, Madison shivered.

'Sorry to interrupt, boss. We're ready for you.'

Catesby nodded. 'I'll be there in a minute. Sorry about this, Miss Morley.'

Madison stood. 'Actually, that's all I came to say, and I don't want to impose.'

'No imposition at all,' Catesby assured her. 'In fact, I'd like you to stay for dinner.'

His hand came to rest on her shoulder. It was all she could do not to flinch under his touch. 'My wife is out, and I was going to have a lonely evening listening to a concert on the radio. Much better to spend it talking about my beautiful home with an interesting and pretty young visitor.'

Madison felt the pressure of his hand increase on her shoulder, pressing her down onto the sofa. 'Well, okay then,' she said reluctantly.

'Good. I shall just conclude this little piece of business, and then my attention will be yours and yours alone.'

Won't that be grand, Madison thought. She drank the rest of the water as the library door closed, her throat tight and dry. Her heart was pumping so wildly it felt as though it were going to climb out of her chest. She sucked in some long breaths and counted to ten before blowing each breath out. She pictured Luke's face, rugged and handsome, as he'd guided the boat back into Penrowan Harbour the other night. *I'm doing this for Luke,* she reminded herself, and immediately felt stronger.

Crossing the library, she opened the door. Definitely time to leave. She could hear Catesby's voice coming from a room down the hall. The temptation was too much for her and she edged along the hallway, straining to pick up on what Catesby was saying.

Suddenly, she felt herself being hoisted into the air as a beefy arm wrapped itself around her middle. She let out a cry.

'What have we here?' Muscles asked.

Madison struggled against him. 'Let me go,' she said, adopting an outraged tone.

The door down the hall flew open and Catesby appeared. 'What's going on?'

'Found her snooping in the hallway, trying to listen in,' Muscles said.

'I was doing no such thing!' Madison said, her tone rising in indignation. 'I was simply looking for the bathroom.'

'Really, Miss Morley! How terribly predictable. Bring her in here.'

Madison struggled ineffectually against the bulk of Muscles as she found herself being carried along. The room was small and hot and crammed with beefy security men.

'Put her in the corner.'

Muscles dropped her into an upholstered chair.

Madison leapt up immediately. 'I need to leave, Mr Catesby. I shall return tomorrow with my grandfather.' Muscles blocked her path.

'Sit down, Miss Morley,' Catesby said.

'No. Please tell your ... man to get out of my way.'

'I have no intention of letting you leave, Miss Morley. I know you're here on false pretences. It was a convincing enough story, I grant you. I may even have believed you if it hadn't been for the fact your grandfather was spotted on the sun deck of Rock Cottage yesterday morning. Rather gives the lie to him having been in Oxford these past few days.'

'You must be mistaken,' Madison said, trying not to let on how shaken she was.

'My men don't make mistakes like that. They even thought they caught a glimpse of Miranda at a second-floor window. Is that likely?'

'Impossible,' Madison replied smartly. 'Seeing as how no one in the village knows where she is.'

'Nice try, Miss Morley, but the jig is up, as they say. Now please sit down. You may find what I have to say to my men of interest to you.'

Madison folded her arms defiantly and stood her ground.

Catesby tutted. 'As you wish,' he said dismissively, and turned back to the assembled group. 'Now that Miss Morley has chosen to grace us with her presence, our priorities have changed. I want the house put on lock-down as from now. No one in or out without my say-so.'

'You don't want us to patrol the grounds?' asked Muscles.

Catesby shook his head. 'There's no need when we have the delightful Miss Morley for company. She's given us the whip hand, albeit unintentionally on her part, I'm sure.'

Madison watched the men depart. Feeling suddenly weary, she backed into the armchair behind her and gratefully sat down.

'Tired, my dear?' Catesby asked, amused.

Catesby's mocking tone cut through Madison's fog of tiredness. She snapped her head upright from where she had been resting it against the wing of the armchair. 'No, I'm fine,' she replied defiantly.

'I doubt that,' Catesby scoffed. 'I dissolved enough sleeping pills in your water to knock out an elephant, and you are considerably smaller than an elephant.'

Madison's eyelids felt as though they had lead weights attached to them. She fought to stay awake. 'Why?' It was the only word she could manage.

'Because I knew you were lying to me the minute you opened your mouth. The question, as you so succinctly put it, is why? Why now? Why here? Have they found the Spanish galleon?'

Madison's head lolled as she gave in to the gentle caress of sleep. The sharp sting of Catesby's hand against her cheek brought her back with a jolt. Tears of shock and pain filled her eyes as her drugged brain plodded to catch up with the situation in which she now found herself.

'Have they found it? Have they found the galleon's treasure?' Catesby's eyes were crazed. He was leaning over her so close that Madison could see the pulse in his temple throbbing.

She smiled and closed her eyes. 'Shouldn't have drugged me.' She licked her lips, her eyes still tightly shut. 'Not if you wanted to question me.' The sentences had taken all her residual energy. Madison flopped back against the seat, feeling herself being pulled deeper by the waves of sleep.

'I don't want to question you, you stupid woman! I want to hold you to ransom for the treasure. I'm going to tuck you away somewhere cold and dark and tell Miranda, Luke and your precious grandfather that they can have you back in exchange for the treasure from the Spanish galleon, and if they don't come up with the goods before high tide tomorrow night, it'll be bye-bye Madison Morley.'

Madison heard the words, but couldn't process them or summon up the strength to respond. She thought of Luke's kiss and smiled dreamily.

'You won't be smiling like that for long where you're going, Miss Morley.'

* * *

Luke paced to and fro. He should have taken Madison with him. However

269

difficult it might have made life, at least they would have been together. He'd asked her if she had the crazy idea of following him and she'd said no. He should have guessed she had another crazy idea. He squeezed his hands into fists. The thought of Madison at Teddy Catesby's mercy made his blood run cold.

'You'll wear that carpet out, lad,' Kathryn said.

Luke threw her a look. If Catesby was capable of medicating his own aunt and holding her prisoner, what would he do to someone to whom he had no personal connection? Luke knew his feelings for Madison were totally out of proportion given the amount of time they had spent together, but he had felt his heart soar the first moment he'd laid eyes on her. There had been something about the contradiction of her cool tone and warm eyes that had drawn him in, and her gravitational pull had held him close ever since.

His mother, the Professor and Miranda were discussing the practicalities of calling the police, but all Luke could do was remember how Madison had looked as he'd waved goodbye to her. Her sunny smile had lit up her face, and as she'd turned to walk away, the wind had caught her long auburn hair, sending it out in streaks. His gaze had travelled down to her narrow waist and cute bottom encased in tight denim. The panic in his heart was almost a physical pain.

He looked up, surprised at the sound of an impatient knock at the door. Striding across the room, Luke threw it open. The last person in the world he expected to see was standing in the street: Teddy Catesby.

'You!' Luke roared. Without thinking, he grabbed the man's shirt with one hand and, putting his arm across Catesby's throat, drove him backwards across the street and into the wall of the opposite cottage. 'If you've hurt her, I swear to God — '

'Luke!' It was his mother's voice, calling him off.

'Get your hands off me, Ryder! It's

Miranda I've come to talk to.'

'Where's Madison?'

'Safe. For now …'

'You …' Luke drew back his closed fist. Catesby braced himself ready for the blow. Luke felt a soft hand close around his fist. He turned to look into Miranda's concerned eyes.

'Let him go, Luke. We need to hear what he has to say.'

Luke knew she was right, but how good it would feel to give vent to his frustrations by pummelling this odious man. Miranda squeezed his fist.

'All right!' He let Catesby go but didn't break eye contact.

Catesby straightened his shirt and followed Miranda into the cottage. Luke hadn't bothered to check whether Catesby had his men with him; now he realised he'd come alone.

'Where's my granddaughter?' the Professor demanded.

'Safe. For now. I know you've found the treasure.'

'We haven't,' Miranda said nonchalantly.

'Let's not play games, Aunt. There's a clock ticking. Eight o'clock tomorrow morning I want you to come to Catesby Hall and tell me the location of the treasure. I will then watch while Ryder recovers it for me. As long as I have the treasure by eight o'clock that evening, I'll tell you where Miss Morley is. A fair exchange, I think. Of course, if you want to tell me the location of the treasure now, we can move that time frame up considerably, but I thought you might want the evening to think it over.'

Luke gave him a baleful stare.

'We don't know where the treasure is,' Miranda repeated.

'I don't believe you,' Catesby snapped. 'I gave Madison some of your sedatives, Aunt. Let's just say she talks in her sleep.'

Kathryn's hand was instantly against Luke's chest. 'If you hurt her, I'll come after you,' Luke said.

Catesby laughed. 'I've got mobsters after me. Proper hard men. A word of warning — never gamble with the Russians. You think, in comparison to them, you scare me, Ryder?'

'I should do,' Luke said, glowering at him.

'Russian mobsters?' Miranda shook her head. 'What happened to you?'

'I should've had Catesby Hall, Aunt. Primogeniture. It should've gone to my father and then to me.'

'Your father always knew that wasn't your grandfather's wish, you foolish, arrogant boy. You pursued a lifestyle you could never afford, and when you finally realised that, you decided to steal that to which you have no claim. Your father would be ashamed of you.'

'My father should have fought for my birthright,' he snapped. 'Once I have the treasure, I'll have the means to leave the country, a new face, a new identity. You'll never hear from me again. In case any of you have the bright idea of calling in the police, you should know I'll deny ever having met Madison Morley.'

'Suppose we had a location, but there's no treasure there?' the Professor asked.

'Then you'd better find another way

to come up with enough money to buy me a new life.' He looked at each one of them in turn. 'Once I've got the treasure and I'm clear of the area, I'll ring you. That should give you enough time to reclaim Miss Morley.' Catesby walked to the door. 'I'll leave you to talk it over. A word of warning, though — don't be late tomorrow. Time and tide wait for no man.'

A babble of voices rose as Catesby slammed the door of the cottage behind him. Luke remained silent. His mother's restraining hand had fallen from his chest, but he stayed rooted to the spot. As much as he might like to make mincemeat of Catesby, it wouldn't help. Better to thwart his twisted plans.

He tuned in to the voices around him. The debate seemed to centre on whether they told Catesby the location of the treasure now or waited until morning.

Miranda turned to him. 'What do you think, Luke?'

'We wait,' he said without hesitation. 'To the very last second of the very last minute before we tell him anything.'

'What if there's no treasure down there?' the Professor said quietly. 'I applaud that you worked out it was in the gardener's cottage. I also applaud the fact you located the ancient well. But that doesn't mean there's anything down there. What then?'

'It won't come to that, Professor,' Luke replied. 'Catesby thinks he holds all the cards, but he's overlooked one crucial thing.'

'Which is?' the Professor asked.

Luke checked his watch. It was heading towards nine o'clock. 'He's given us just under twelve hours to find Madison.'

'How can we possibly do that?' Kathryn asked. 'She could be anywhere.'

He shook his head. 'He hasn't had enough time to leave the area, Ma.'

'Luke's right,' the Professor said, seizing Luke's arm. 'Could she be at Catesby Hall in the same room you were held in, Miranda?'

She shook her head. 'He wouldn't risk it. If we called his bluff and brought in the police, the first thing they'd do is search the Hall.'

'Then she's on the grounds some-where,' Luke said. 'Or at one of your properties in the village. When Catesby had her snatched off the street, they took her to old John Parsons' place in Lower Dale. That's as good a place to start as any. Any objection to my carrying out a little breaking and entering, Miranda?'

'I'm the owner,' she said, 'and you have my full permission to break and enter.' She grabbed her coat.

★   ★   ★

It was the cold that woke her. She opened her eyes to be greeted by pitch-black nothingness. Madison swallowed. Her mouth and throat were parched. The darkness was oppressive and utterly ter-rifying. How long had she been asleep? Chilly currents of air worked their way beneath her clothes, making her shiver.

She moved her awareness around her body. She was sitting upright. Her wrists had been tied behind her back. The ties were plastic, tight and strong. She flexed against them but knew immediately it was pointless. She was leaning against something cold and hard. It felt like rock.

She moved her hands down to the floor. She was sitting on more rock. Was she in a cave? She considercd her legs. They were stretched out in front of her. With a shuffle, she dug in her heels and bent her knees. That was interesting. It wasn't rock beneath her heels; it gave way beneath her weight and then became firm. Sand? She continued to move her legs and, using her hands to push at the rock behind her, edged herself up. It was a struggle, hindered as she was by her wrists being tied and the after-effects of the sedative that Catesby had given her, but she managed to lever herself into a half-crouch. She made a concerted effort to stand. With a bang, the top of her head hit rock and she sat down with a thud that jarred her spine, her head spinning.

Panic seized her. 'Help me,' she croaked. Then, clearing her throat, she shouted, 'Help me!' The words seemed to bounce off the rocks, mocking her as they echoed away.

Closing her eyes, Madison tried to remember what Catesby had been saying to her as she had succumbed to the embrace of sleep; something about holding her to ransom.

Her heart was racing, beating wildly. She opened her eyes. The heavy blackness seemed even more awful the second time around. She struggled to breathe, so tight was her chest from the fear. Despite the cold that had woken her, she could feel prickles of perspiration breaking out on her forehead. What was this place?

She counted to ten and then to twenty. *Let your eyes adjust. What might seem like impenetrable blackness may have a glimmer of light in time. What can you smell?* There *was* a smell, a distinct smell. Salty, tangy, sharp. The sea!

Think. It was the cold air that woke you. She felt a draught hitting her left thigh and another knifing around her shoulders. If there were air currents, then this was not a cell, man-made and impossible to break out of; it was a cave. And caves have entrances and exits. She hung on to that thought as she waited for her eyes to adjust.

Surely there had to be a change of light somewhere within her prison, wherever the air flow was emanating from? *Work from top to bottom, left to right, seek it out.* It was there somewhere. It had to be — a subtle shift from utter darkness to a lighter smudge of shadow. She just had to find it and work her way towards it.

Madison inclined her head. What was that noise? 'Hello? Is someone there? Hello? Help me, please!'

She listened intently for a reply. All she could hear was a distant slapping sound. Was that some kind of machine? She edged closer to where she estimated the sound was coming from, praying she wouldn't hit her head again on the low-hanging rock. Twisting round, she flexed her fingers. Her instincts had been right: the rock she was sitting on gave way to sand.

She was just processing the fact that it was damp sand when a trickle of ice-cold seawater ran over the back of her fingers. With a scream, Madison snatched her hand away.

She could feel more water seeping into her prison, running in familiar channels. The bottoms of her trouser legs were growing damp. There was water against her thigh now, just a trickle but growing stronger all the time.

Madison quickly manoeuvred herself back onto the rocky ledge she had started out from. It seemed logically to be the highest point available to her. She crouched there, shivering with the cold and fear. The slapping sound that had so intrigued her earlier now gave flight to her fears. It was the sound of the sea, she realised, rhythmically rising and hitting the rocky outcrop that must be situated somewhere just outside her prison.

The tide was encroaching. What had been a trickle a few minutes ago was a stream now; several, in fact. Just how far did the tide wash into this place? All the way? And then what? Did it rise to her waist? Her neck?

Catesby's words came back to her in all of their heart-stopping terror: 'If they don't come up with the goods before high tide tomorrow night, it'll be bye-bye Madison Morley.'

Catesby had been very precise. High tide tomorrow night. Presumably, only at certain high tides was her cave completely submerged. The question was, how long had she been asleep? Twelve hours, or twenty-four? She simply did not know. Would the tide peak at her neck and then subside to rise to the ceiling the following day, or would the water rush in relentlessly over the next minutes and hours, filling the cave to the ceiling and turning her prison into a watery coffin? She had no way of knowing other than to track the remorselessly rising water and see where it peaked.

Madison redoubled her efforts, struggling against the ties that bound her, screaming for help at the top of her lungs. Surely someone had to hear her? Sound did funny things through rock, didn't it? There was a chance, however slim, that her voice would be bounced and carried all the way to the cliff top, if only someone happened to be walking by at just the right moment. It was fanciful and she knew it, but it was all she had.

*   *   *

The old cottage door had proved to be a sterner test than Luke had anticipated, particularly as his right shoulder was still sore from Miranda's earlier blow. But they had finally gained entry, and he and Miranda had searched the cottage from the attic to the cellar and even the garden, to no avail.

All the other Catesby properties in the village were occupied, so they had reconvened in the kitchen of Rock Cottage to plot their next move. In their absence, Kathryn had made a pot of tea, and they were now all drinking deeply from brightly coloured mugs. What was it about the restorative powers of tea in times of crisis? he wondered.

Miranda was ticking off all the out-buildings at Catesby Hall where Madison might be incarcerated, but something didn't sit right with Luke. Catesby could be a reckless fool, but he wasn't stupid. If they did call in the police, Catesby had to know they would search the Hall and the grounds from top to bottom. Luke drained his mug and banged it down on the kitchen table.

'We're missing something,' he said, and raked a hand through his hair. So desperate was he about Madison's plight that he could hardly think straight, and yet she needed him to do just that. *Concentrate, man!* 'Why eight o'clock tomorrow morning? Why not seven or nine? And why eight o'clock tomorrow night? He was adamant he had to have the treasure by then, make his escape, and then he'd ring us. That should give us enough time. That's what he said. Why is the time so important?'

'Maybe he has a plane to catch,' Kathryn mused.

'Eight in the morning and eight at night.' Luke thumped his forehead with the palm of his hand. 'Of course! He said it himself. Time and tide wait for no man.' Luke looked at each of his companions. 'Time and *tide*,' he repeated.

'Dear God.' The Professor brought his hand up to his mouth.

'He's put her in the Swiss-cheese caves,' Miranda said, meeting Luke's gaze.

He nodded grimly. The Swiss-cheese caves, as the locals called them, were actually a series of caves beneath Penrowan Point. Luke could remember his mother's warning ringing in his and his brother's ears when they were boys: 'Them caves are a death trap. Little boys go playing in there and never come out. My mother told me about a boy in her grandfather's time. Young Tommy Jolliffe went to explore there and he was never seen again. Only seven, he was. Sometimes when the gales are blowing, people fancy they can still hear Tommy's cries for help.'

Naturally, their mother's warning had only made the caves seem even more enticing. Sensing that his boys might be more brave than sensible, their father had taken them in hand. Skimming the water in his motorboat on a bright summer's day, he had taken them to the Swiss-cheese caves. Securing the boat, he had helped both boys onto the rocks, and they had spent happy hours exploring the caves. As the water around their feet had swirled and eddied, rising fast, their father had steered them back towards the entrance to the cave complex.

'You see how quickly the tide rushes in?' he had asked once they were safely back in the boat.

The boys nodded solemnly. They could see the entrance to the first cave and how the water was already lapping at the walls.

'Some of the smaller caves at the back are death traps. Your mother was right — the water rises so quickly that if you get stuck, there's a very real chance you won't get out, no matter how strong a swimmer you think you are. The sea is merciless, remember that.'

Luke's face was grim as he recalled his

father's stark warning. He'd been right; the sea was merciless. It had taken his father and his brother from him. He'd be damned if he'd let it take Madison too.

'You can't go alone,' his mother said. 'Please, Luke.'

'I'll give Charlie a shout,' he said. 'He'll help me. We'll go prepared, Ma. Lights, ropes, breathing apparatus. Although I'm hoping we won't need that,' he added quickly, catching the Professor's worried look.

'It's the vernal equinox,' the Professor said, shutting his eyes against the horror of his thoughts. 'The highest of high tides.'

Luke nodded grimly. 'Tomorrow it'll be at its peak. There's still time. Can you get Charlie for me, Ma? I'll ready the boat and the equipment. Tell him to meet me at the harbour.'

Kathryn nodded, leaving immediately.

'I'll get her back, Professor. I promise,' Luke said.

'I trust you, my boy. God speed.'

★   ★   ★

Madison was so tired. More tired than she could ever remember. Her limbs dragged as she worked against the strong currents pushing and pulling her. The water had reached her collarbone now as she paddled. She had found a spot near the entrance to the cave where the water was pouring in and around a large boulder which presumably Catesby's goons had rolled into place. There was no way round or over it. To stand with her feet on the bottom meant submerging herself totally, but she did it over and over again, trying to anchor her feet into the sandy floor, bracing her back against the boulder and pushing with all her might against its bulk. When she could hold her breath no longer, she would bob to the surface and cry for help between gulping lungfuls of sweet air, before starting the whole process again. There had to be a way out. She couldn't just wait and hope the water peaked before it drowned her.

She forced herself to cry for help once

more, her teeth chattering with the cold as she did so. Hypothermia was likely to get her before the water did. The thought made her angry. Angrier than she had ever been. Angrier even than she had been at Will over his affair. This was not how her life was going to end. There was so much to live for. People who loved her. And Luke. There was Luke. She thought of his ruggedly handsome face, his rangy limbs, his strength. How she needed a little bit of that right now.

Readying herself to dive once more, she marshalled her flagging limbs for another supreme effort and tried to ignore the fact that the seawater had started to lap against her chin.

$$\star \quad \star \quad \star$$

Luke hardly had to swim at all; so forceful was the current of the relentlessly rising tide that it carried him swiftly into the cave system. He had a rope secured round his waist and a powerful torch in his hand. There was an oxygen tank strapped to the back of his wetsuit but the mouthpiece hung around his neck. He didn't want to use valuable air that he might need later. There was still plenty of clearance between the water and the roof of the cave system, which boosted his spirits.

He could feel Charlie steadily feeding out the rope from the boat positioned in the mouth of the caves. He trusted Charlie with his life — was doing just that, he realised. Charlie was a good bloke and Luke was relieved that he was with him.

Luke knew that the smaller caves at the back of the complex were likely to be where he would find Madison. He was aware from his exploration with his brother, under the watchful eye of their father, that the sandy floor dipped significantly towards the back end of the cave system, and that while he might have good height clearance where he was, it was likely to be significantly reduced where Madison was. He cursed Catesby.

'Madison!' he yelled. 'Madison!' He paused momentarily to listen for a response, worried that his movement through the water would cover the sound of her reply. But there was nothing, only the whistling of the wind and the slap of the seawater. 'Hang on, Maddy! I'm coming to get you.'

* * *

Madison's lungs were on fire despite the bone-chilling cold. She couldn't fight it any longer. She had to rise and take a breath. She choked and coughed as she took in a mouthful of seawater. Boy, the water was getting high now! Surely it had to peak soon?

She tilted her head back to take another breath, seawater sloshing into her ears as she did so. Her muscles were cramping with the effort, exacerbated by the lack of food and drink. How much more did she have left to give? She already felt as though she were running on empty.

' ... son!'

Was she imaging things now, or had

she heard a voice? She strained to listen, lifting herself as high as she could above the water, hampered by her hands still tied behind her back.

'Madison!'

She wasn't imagining it. 'Luke! Oh my God, Luke! I'm here!' She paddled furiously to maintain her position, fighting against the current which all the time was trying to push her back against the far wall.

'Madison!'

'Luke!'

'Keep talking, your voice will guide me to you!'

She didn't need to be told twice. She started shouting his name over and over again, until at last she could hear his voice loud and clear. She sensed he was just the other side of the boulder. She gave him a quick description of her situation, though she left out how cold she was and how badly her legs were cramping.

'Righto! We'll have you out of there in a jiffy.'

He sounded so confident. She let his

confidence seep through her, filling her up.

'Maddy, I'm going to need you to try to push the rock one more time. The biggest push you've got in you. I just need it to pivot ever so slightly and I can roll it aside. Do you think you can do that?'

'Yes!'

'Dive on three. You push on five and I'll push on seven.'

'Okay.'

'One … two … three.'

Madison sank down, adopting the familiar stance, bracing herself against the rock, anchoring her feet. She heaved with all her might, her thighs shaking with the effort. Was it wishful thinking, or had the rock moved slightly? For good measure, she pushed again. But then her lungs were burning and she had to rise for air.

'Great job, Maddy! We're almost there.'

She could hear Luke grunting with the effort of trying to manhandle the boulder. Suddenly there was gap, a thin sliver. She could see it through the refracted light of the beam of Luke's torch.

His hand pushed through. 'Maddy?'

She turned and grabbed it, sobbing with delight.

'A few more inches and you'll be out of there.'

Madison knew it would take more than a few inches. She wasn't that skinny! But his optimism was just what she needed.

'My God, Madison! You're freezing!'

'Yes,' she said, her teeth chattering once more.

'You've got to let go of my hand, sweetheart. I need them both if I'm going to get you out of there.' Reluctantly, she did so.

A few moments later, the gap was wide enough to pass the torch through. Securing it in her mouth, Madison swung the beam around, studying her prison cell. It had seemed larger in the pitch black.

Putting her hands on the boulder, Madison pushed with all her might. They would do this together. Teamwork.

Sure enough, she felt the boulder give a little and then a little more.

Suddenly it tumbled to one side and she swam through the opening, straight into Luke's arms.

14

A cloudless blue sky greeted the party standing in front of the gardener's cottage the following morning. The Professor, Miranda and Luke were ranged on one side, Catesby and two of his goons on the other.

'This the spot?' Catesby asked eagerly.

'Thirty paces from the front of the cottage,' Miranda confirmed, and pointed to where Luke was standing.

'Good.' Catesby motioned for one of his goons to hand him the shovel he had been holding. Lifting it in the air, he threw it at Luke, who caught it deftly.

'Start digging, Ryder, and don't stop until you've recovered all my lovely treasure.' Catesby folded his arms, a smug grin on his face.

Luke plunged the shovel into the grass then leaned nonchalantly against its handle.

'What are you doing?' Catesby asked, bemused.

'I don't feel much like digging today,' Luke said. 'I had a late night.'

'Is this some kind of joke?' Catesby demanded.

'I didn't get a lot of sleep.'

'Then you should have known better! Seeing as how your girlfriend's life depends on it,' Catesby replied tersely.

'Ah, but you see, that's just it,' Madison said as she emerged through the front door of the cottage. 'He was up half the night rescuing me.'

'How...' Catesby began, bewildered. Then, at the sight of police officers pouring out of the cottage, he turned, preparing to flee, only to come face to face with more police officers approaching across the glade. Madison watched as a group of them wrestled Catesby and his men to the ground.

'What was it you said to me?' she asked. 'Oh yes! The jig is up.'

Luke put his arm around her shoulders.

'Well and truly, I'd say. Wouldn't you, Teddy?'

As the officers read the men their rights, Catesby looked back over his shoulder. 'Did you really find it?'

'Yes,' Miranda replied. 'And my friends are going to help me recover it.'

⋆   ⋆   ⋆

It took two days to lift the floor of the gardener's cottage and get the equipment in place to hoist the treasure from its centuries-long hiding place. They discovered that Cornelius Catesby had been a very clever man. Aware that the water table might rise as well as fall, he had made a platform to fit across the well a third of the way down. Upon it he had stacked ten leather sacks, tied at the mouth with rope. Each one was full to the brim of silver pieces of eight.

Now, as the sun set on the second day, the group toasted their treasure hunt with champagne on the deck of Rock Cottage.

'I just wanted to say thank you to all

of you,' Miranda said. 'I am so sorry for what my nephew put you through, Madison, and I'll do everything in my power to make it up to you, I promise.'

'There's no need; I'm fine,' Madison assured her. She smiled at her grandfather.

'Gave me a terrible fright, Sticky Stick,' he said, hugging her to him.

'I'm fine,' she said again, releasing him. 'Thanks to Luke.'

Luke's arm snaked around her waist as his warm lips connected with hers.

As she drew back, Madison could see Kathryn beaming. 'I always knew you two were just right for each other,' she said.

'Plain as the nose on your face,' Miranda agreed, nodding sagely.

'Pity it took the two of you so long to figure it out,' Kathryn said, laughing. 'Still, you got there in the end.'

The Professor raised his glass. 'To Madison and Luke.'

The others echoed his toast.

'To the Spanish galleon and her treasure, surely?' Luke countered.

'Safely under lock and key now, being

counted,' Miranda said with a contented sigh. 'The initial estimate is somewhere just north of a million pounds.' Luke whistled.

'When do you get it back?' Madison asked.

'Under the Treasure Act ...' Miranda paused and chuckled. 'Who would've thought there even was such a thing? Anyway, it needs to be cleaned and then properly valued and analysed. And then, as the landowner, I have the right to sell it. The red tape will doubtless take a while.'

'And Teddy?' Madison asked.

'He's been charged with two counts of false imprisonment.'

'Should've been attempted murder,' Luke cut in.

'He maintained the cave would never have completely filled even at the highest tide. Others in the cave system do, but not the one he put Madison in. It gives me some hope that my nephew isn't completely heartless. Nevertheless, he'll be spending a substantial amount of time in jail. And I'll be busy putting my house back in order and making amends to everyone in the village whom my nephew has upset.'

'That could take a while,' Luke said.

'Indeed.' Miranda gave a rueful smile.

'If you'd all excuse us, I'd like a few minutes alone with Madison,' Luke said.

Sunny smiles greeted his words. Taking Madison's hand, Luke guided her through to the lounge, shutting the door against galloping ears.

'The last few days have been crazy,' Madison said. 'Who would have thought we would have found ourselves caught up in a centuries-old treasure hunt for lost Spanish silver?'

Luke nodded.

'Is it always like that round here?'

'Oh, no! Sometimes it gets really wild,' Luke replied with a grin.

Madison laughed. He rejoiced in the sound, committing it to memory. As he turned to face her, the speech he had been rehearsing was suddenly lost to him. 'Madison, I…' he foundered. Then he snatched the painting of the storm-tossed Penrowan Harbour from the wall and offered it to her. 'I want you to have this to remember us all by, as well as the painting of Penrowan Point.'

Madison's eyes widened in surprise. 'Remember you all by? Why? Do you think I'm going somewhere?'

Luke smiled. 'Women like you are always going somewhere, Maddy. Big dreams, big plans, small villages. In my experience, they don't mix well.'

'As we've already established, you don't get out much,' she replied tartly.

He laughed. 'That's true. Please take the painting.' He offered it to her, and when she didn't take it, he stood it against the sofa between them.

'You know how much I love this painting,' Madison said, sinking to her haunches to fully appreciate it. 'And I'm honoured you're willing to part with it.'

Biting down on his emotions, Luke took a step away from her. 'I don't want us to promise each other we'll make it work, Maddy, however much I might want to. Long-distance relationships are always doomed…'

'This is you talking from a position of huge experience on the subject,' she angled with a smile as she stood.

'Stop making light of this, Maddy. You're not making it easy for me.'

'Good! I don't want it to be easy. You're trying to say goodbye to me.'

'I just don't want either of us to get hurt again.'

'Neither do I. My grandfather has accepted Miranda's offer to recuperate at Catesby Hall after his op. He's going to pack up and move all of his research papers to the library there. I'll need to be on hand to help him with that. And then, of course, there'll be Teddy's trial. You won't get rid of me that easily.'

'It won't be enough for you,' Luke said, even though the words almost choked him.

'You're right, it won't. Which is why I'm going to lease one of the shops in the village and turn it into an art gallery: paintings on the ground floor and sculpture and *objets d'art* on the first floor. And before you say anything, I'm not doing this for you. I'm doing it for me. The thought of having my own space, to organise and curate how I wish, will be a dream come true.'

Luke smiled. She was an irresistible force and he could see there was no point arguing with her. In truth, he didn't want to. His heart was singing at the prospect of Madison Morley being in his life from this moment on. 'I'll take this back then,' he said with a grin, his hand on the painting.

She slapped his hand away. 'I think not.'

He took her in his arms and kissed her deeply.

'It's no good trying to distract me,' Madison said.

'Where are you planning on living while you plot your art empire?' he asked archly.

'Miranda says I can stay at the Hall, but I'm hoping a handsome local painter may let me move in.'

'Really?' Luke's eyes twinkled. 'Zero

percent commission on any of my paintings sold in your gallery.'

'Done,' she responded.

'You have been,' he replied smartly. He hoisted the painting of Penrowan Harbour back on the wall. 'I guess now that you'll be moving in, you can bring your painting with you,' he said by way of explanation.

Madison laughed as she watched him fix the painting back on the wall. Settling her arms around his waist, she leaned her head on his shoulder with a contented sigh.

'We'll leave the days of broken hearts behind us, Maddy,' Luke vowed.

'Absolutely,' she agreed.

Her grandfather had told her that Penrowan would be good for her soul, and so it had proved. Luke Ryder wasn't bad, either.

We do hope that you have enjoyed reading this large print book.

Did you know that all of our titles are available for purchase?

We publish a wide range of high quality large print books including:
Romances, Mysteries, Classics
General Fiction
Non Fiction and Westerns

Special interest titles available in large print are:
The Little Oxford Dictionary
Music Book, Song Book
Hymn Book, Service Book

Also available from us courtesy of Oxford University Press:
Young Readers' Dictionary
(large print edition)
Young Readers' Thesaurus
(large print edition)

For further information or a free brochure, please contact us at:
Ulverscroft Large Print Books Ltd.,
The Green, Bradgate Road, Anstey,
Leicester, LE7 7FU, England.
Tel: (00 44) **0116 236 4325**
Fax: (00 44) **0116 234 0205**